凱信企管

用對的方法充實自己，
讓人生變得更美好！

凱信企管

用對的方法充實自己，
讓人生變得更美好！

引導式英語練習班

式練習班

聽說讀寫大量多元習題，打造英語力

序

　　學好英文一直是許多人的重要課題，然而，英文總學不好，也是大多數人很頭痛的問題。尤其，身處地球村的我們，英語確實是我們最需要掌握的語言工具之一。

　　大部分的人都非常清楚英語的重要性，不論是為了讀書、工作或生活上的需求，具備英文溝通能力已經變成是最基本的必備技能。但為什麼在我們經歷了國中、高中甚至大學近十年的英語教育之後，英文程度卻是連最簡單的溝通都有問題，甚至更慘，根本不敢開口說？相信，你一定也有同樣的困擾與疑問：我過去十年的英文真的都白學了嗎？

　　根據我多年的觀察，有眾多的英語學習者因升學、考試的緣故，強迫自己背了許多艱深的單字、讓自己有能力書寫結構嚴謹的文章，然而，他們到了國外卻發現，不知道該如何開口跟鄰居聊天、處理生活大小事，因而十分受挫。原因在於他們所學的那些艱澀的單字，在一般的對話中不一定能派得上用場。「但我又不住在英語國家，生活英語要怎麼學？」相信有不少人都有這個疑問。因此，本書除了要你利用十年來的所學，讓你用溫故再知新的方式學習之外，同時更著眼於生活中的細節，以此衍生出許多和日常社交有關的題材。試想：要是只讀課本卻看不懂廣告標語，或是講英語的朋友跟你打招呼而你卻一頭霧水，那下了多年工夫所學的英語不就白費了嗎？所以，本書從報導、銀行理財表單、社區文宣中截取閱讀題材，貼近生活實際。聽力內容也是從日常話題中取材，若是精熟聽力測驗中的對話，就更能幫助你，讓你在和房仲業者打電話、向醫生說明病情、戀愛交往或是與人閒聊時無往不利。

本書除了有各式各樣有趣的題材之外，練習也十分充足。每個unit中有五到八個part，而每個part中有三到十一個長短不一的練習題，有選擇、搭配、造句、作文等各種題型，利用故事情節讓各個題目之間相關聯，使學習者更能藉此從各個角度思考、分析文章脈絡，並且做全面的練習。此外，每個單元結束後，還另外補充一篇聽力測驗作為總復習。相信學習者若認真地攻讀本書，不僅能全面提升英語能力，也能學會抓重點、做筆記的技巧，在各個領域都十分受用。

　　當你英文的閱讀能力及寫作能力都相對提升之後，若是想要增加口語能力的學習者，又該如何使用本書呢？本書特別在書中適時的為學習者安排了口說練習，並在每個單元的最後附上該單元的MP3音檔完整內容的文字呈現，讓讀者能根據指示，朗讀習題或是兩人一組練習對話。因此，不必擔心自學英語會練不到口語，只要跟著這本書，一樣可以拉親朋好友一起來開口說英語。

　　十年不白學！請再給自己一次機會，只要有心認真學習，本書一定讓你有信心，這次英語一定可以學得好，更能開口說。祝福各位在學習完本書後，英語實力都能更上一層樓，並且能在日常生活中享受英語溝通無障礙的便利！

使用說明

別再低頭苦背字典，
抬起頭張開口親身體驗世界吧！

01 10年英語不白學，用暖身練習找回零星記憶

在正式開始學習之前先來點暖身吧！讓眼熟的英文，先重新啟動你記憶深處曾經學習過的英語，找回英文語感，建立學習自信。該部分根據每個單元的內容設計了開放式練習題，讓你可以先動動腦，根據自己的想像力及書上提示填入適當的答案，為接下來的學習做準備。（例如p.12）

02 加強社交英語理解溝通能力，道地英語脫口而出！

本書根據閱讀和聽力測驗內容設計了多種題型，讓學習者能透過題目學習判斷文章大意、抓住重點、提出並回答問題。閱讀選題從報導、銀行理財到社區文宣，題材豐富。聽力內容也是從日常話題中取材，如果熟練聽力測驗的對話，就更能幫助你在跟醫生說明病情、與朋友或陌生人閒聊時無往不利。除此之外，每單元有5-8組練習題，包含用來分析文章和對話的標題判斷、簡答、填表格等題目，根據文章大意出題的填空、選擇、搭配等題目，更有造句、寫摘要等練習長句子書寫的題目，好好練習必定能完美掌握英語聽、讀、寫的技巧。（例如p.14）

03 社交英語無師自通，你一定還想知道更多！

除了每個單元教的內容以外，書中會不定時補充延伸學習的小知識，讓你可以思考：怎樣問問題比較有禮貌？怎樣回答不會跟不上潮流？哪些問句其實只是在寒暄，認真回答反而會顯得很可笑？你會藉由書中的這些提示，進而更了解英語的表達方式，更貼近英美文化！（例如p.43）

04 拒當英文句點王，換你練習開口說說看！

學完一個主題，填了很多答案、寫了很多句子，但是不是覺得似乎沒練習到口語呢？別擔心，書中會適時出現讓學習者練習口說的部分，當你遇到這個練習時，就

請你根據指示，勇敢大聲地說出來吧！從朗讀自己寫的答案，跟著音檔一起唸到兩人一組的練習，讓你無論發音、音調都能面面俱到，開口就是漂亮道地的用語，從此不怕跟英語人士打交道！（例如p.27）

05 學習進度確認清單：學完這一單元，你就可以……

終於學習完一個單元了！每個單元的最後都有列重點清單，羅列了在該單元應該學習到的核心技能，快來勾勾看，檢查一下你是不是都已經掌握了呢？如果清單上有空著沒打勾的選項，務必要回頭再復習一遍！（例如p.66）

06 社交英語無師自通，道地英語該怎麼寫？！

確認當前練習的單元自己都學會了以後，就來試著寫一篇文章吧，若想學以致用，寫作是一個很好的訓練和驗證方式。因此，請在這個部分根據題目指示，發揮想像力，並運用已經學會的種種技巧，撰寫一篇篇生動有趣的短文吧！（例如p.66-68）

07 單元總復習！

結束一個單元後，仍然意猶未盡、還想練習？或是發現自己錯得有點多，覺得不安心？每單元的總復習都提供一篇精選的聽力測驗，幫你重點回顧整個單元，補上疏漏之處，打盡漏網之魚！（例如p.69）

08 MP3音檔內容完整看！

每個單元的最後都收錄了所有音檔的完整文字，方便學習者做完題目以後可以研讀，找出聽錯的地方加以注記之外，不熟的語彙要查辭典並作筆記，方能加深英文記憶。朗讀書本裡的對話文字，也是訓練口語的好方法，你也可以和親朋好友一同模擬對話，一起增進英語實力。（例如p.71）

09 外師親錄強效學習MP3，社交英語聽力口說同步訓練！

每個單元充份利用MP3內容，藉由反覆的收聽做測驗練習，不僅能加強聽力，同時更能跟著一起開口讀，訓練一口發音漂亮的口語。（例如p.22 Track 001）

目錄

Unit 3 健康 Health

Unit 4 人生百態 People

Unit 1 社區 Local Community

Part 1 社交英語無師自通，道地的「居住場所或區域」該怎麼說？
Part 2 社交英語無師自通，道地的「用電話詢問住處細節」該怎麼說？
Part 3 社交英語無師自通，道地的「社區內的各種設施」該怎麼說？
Part 4 社交英語無師自通，道地的「各種設施的功用」該怎麼說？
Part 5 社交英語無師自通，道地的「社區安全計劃」該怎麼說？
Part 6 社交英語無師自通，道地的「處理銀行事務」該怎麼說？
Part 7 社交英語無師自通，道地的「初來乍到遇到的情況」該怎麼說？
Part 8 社交英語無師自通，道地的「描述我的新家」該怎麼寫？

★ 第一單元總復習
★ MP3音檔內容完整看

Unit 1 社區

Local Community

你是住在學校宿舍還是公寓呢？或者擁有自己的獨棟別墅？這些都是組成社區的基本要素之一。現在社會越來越進步，我們所居住的社區裡面，服務機構和設備也越來越完善。世界上還有哪些種類的房屋？如何了解一個社區？讓我們一起看看吧。

十年英語不白學，「我們所居住的場所」你怎麼說？

我們可能住在學校宿舍（dormitories）、公寓（flats）或者別墅（villas）裡，而這些也是城市（city）或鄉村（country）的組成部分。看看下面方框中的話，找出用來描述他們所居住的場所或區域的單字或片語。

I live in a busy area.
It's really interesting.

There's a real sense of community where I live. Many people live on the same housing estate for the whole of their lives.

I live in quite a rough district.
There's often trouble after the pubs close!

The neighbourhood I live in is rather quiet.

Our house is in a pleasant suburb of the city.

My room is on the campus so it's very convenient.

We live in the country, in an isolated farmhouse in the middle of some fields.

I'm lucky enough to have a flat in the town centre.

透過閱讀上頁的對話框，你是否已經鎖定了目標單字或片語呢？請把這些單字或片語寫在下面橫線上。我已經為你寫好第一個了！

✏️ 寫出用來描述居住場所或區域的單字或片語。

area,

社交英語無師自通，你一定還想知道更多！

中國人喜歡說 "living in the countryside"（住在鄉下），英美國家的人又是怎麼表達「住在鄉下」呢？他們通常會說 "living out of town" 或 "living in the country"。

提示與解析

描述居住場所或區域的單字或片語：

housing estate, district, neighbourhood, suburb, campus, country, town centre

這些單字或片語都可以用來描述人們所居住的區域。要注意句子中出現的介系詞！其中，"in" 是最常用來搭配這些詞或片語的介系詞，而 "on" 後面有可能接 "housing estate" 或 "campus" 等詞彙。

無論是住在哪一個區域當中，你都算是住在一個 "community" 之中。"community" 直接翻譯就是「社區」的意思，但和中文所說的「社區」又並非完全相同。在這個單元中，我們會好好探究 "community" 到底有哪些含意。

Part 1——
社交英語無師自通，
道地的「居住場所或區域」該怎麼說？

　　年輕的工程師高斌剛抵達英國，因為他的公司派他到曼徹斯特（Manchester）出差六個月。這六個月的住宿他得自己想辦法，所以他正在煩惱要找怎樣的房子來住。

　　在中國，過去最常見的房屋種類就是四合院，現在則是一個個街區的公寓大樓。此外，中國與世界其他地方還有很多不同種類的房屋：detached houses（獨立式住宅），terraced houses（排屋公寓），bungalows（小平房）等。下頁的方框中有許多不同種類的房屋，方框下方提供了它們的定義。請在每個定義旁邊寫下相對應的房屋名稱，並觀察這些房屋的圖片，將每種房屋的名稱寫在對應圖片下方的橫線上。

　　將房屋種類的不同表達分別與其定義搭配。

a detached house	*a semi-detached house*	*a terraced house*	*a housing estate*
a block of flats	*a cottage*	*a bungalow*	*a caravan*	*a high-rise / tower block*

❶ _____ : a house which is part of a continuous row of houses all of the same type in one block

❷ _____ : a small house, especially in the country

❸ _____ : a building with several storeys and separate flats

❹ _____ : a temporary home on wheels which can be moved from place to place

❺ _____ : a house which is totally separate from other houses

❻ _____ : a tall building which has many storeys

❼ _____ : an area where lots of houses are grouped together

⑧ _____ : a house which is joined to another house by one wall that they share

⑨ _____ : a house with only one storey

將房屋種類的名稱寫在相應圖片下方的橫線上，其中前三個已為你寫好了。

❶ a block of flats	❷ a terraced house	❸ a detached house
❹	❺	❻
❼	❽	❾

提示與解析

定義搭配：

1 a terraced house   **2** a cottage

3 a block of flats   **4** a caravan

5 a detached house   **6** a high-rise / tower block

7 a housing estate   **8** a semi-detached house

9 a bungalow

請注意，a high-rise / tower block 和 a block of flats不一樣！前者是有很多層樓的一棟高樓（裡面通常會有電梯），而後者通常不會很高。

圖片名稱：

4 a caravan   **6** a semi-detached house   **8** a cottage

5 a bungalow   **7** a housing estate   **9** a high-rise / tower block

十年英語不白學，「房屋廣告的相關縮寫」就這麼寫

　　高斌問了許多人，怎樣才能找到最適合自己的房子，於是有人建議他看當地報紙的租房專欄（Accommodation to Let）。高斌覺得，他比較想住 "house" 或 "flat"，最好在市中心或方便的車站附近，並且想和其他人合租，因為一個人住可能會寂寞。此外，他希望新家最好配備家具，而且可以做飯，因為他不想天天在外吃飯。他知道曼徹斯特的冬天又濕又冷，所以他還希望新家有空調。他的預算是一個月600英鎊至700英鎊，視瓦斯費和電費等是否需要另外計算而定。也就是說，如果瓦斯費和電費等雜費需要額外算，每個月租金最好不超過600英鎊；如果租金包含瓦斯費和電費等雜費，則可以接受700英鎊的月租。

高斌看了一些廣告，如下所示。你會發現，這些廣告中使用了很多縮寫（為了省空間，因為報紙版面空間珍貴，字字都是金錢）。高斌研究了很久，才弄清楚這些縮寫代表什麼意思。那麼，現在請閱讀廣告，並在廣告後表格中的空白處寫下相應縮寫部分的完整形式。第一項我已經幫你填好了！

閱讀廣告，並寫下縮寫部分的完整形式。

Ad. 1

To LET: Exc. 1st fl. flat; conv. for buses, shops etc., dbl. b., fitted k & b, gar., gas c.h. unfurn., prof. person / couple preferred. No pets. £300 pw. Tel: Happy Flats Agency, 3035847

Ad. 2

FOR RENT: part-furn. modern flat, of a high standard, avail. now in new city centre bl. Would suit single prof. person. £240 pw. Tel: 3424673

Ad. 3

AVAILABLE NOW: Close to buses and shops, two single rooms in comfortable shared house. Fully equipped. £160 pw. inc. bills. Non-smokers. Male pref. Call 3075219 for details.

Ad. 4

TO LET: conv. 3 b. furn. flat with gar., fitted k & b, suit 3 gentlemen sharing. Rent: £450 (£150 each) pw., excluding bills. Tel: 3622179.

Ad. 5

FOR RENT: single furn. room in family house, extremely clean and well maintained. No cooking facilities. Chinese students pref. £150 + bills. Tel: 3760417

Ad. 6

AVAILABLE NOW: Bedsit, recently converted and decorated. No cooking. Shared b., female pref. £100 pw. Contact: Happy Flats Agency, 3035847

① exc.: *excellent*	**②** conv.:
③ k & b:	**④** dbl. b.:
⑤ (un)furn.:	**⑥** part-furn.:
⑦ pref. :	**⑧** prof.:
⑨ inc.:	**⑩** p.w. / pw.:
⑪ c. h.:	**⑫** avail.:
⑬ bl. :	**⑭** 1st fl.:
⑮ gar.:	**⑯** tel.:

提示與解析

② convenient	**③** kitchen and bathroom
④ double bedroom	**⑤** (un)furnished
⑥ part-furnished	**⑦** preferred / preferable
⑧ professional	**⑨** included / including
⑩ per week	**⑪** central heating
⑫ available	**⑬** block (or building)
⑭ first floor	**⑮** garage (or garden)
⑯ telephone (number)	

你有沒有發現第13項和第15項有兩個可能的答案？這就是縮寫可能會產生的不便之處，因為大家有時會解讀成不同的意思。所以要搞清楚這些縮寫到底代表什麼意思，最快的方式就是直接打電話去問！

十年英語不白學，「對住宿的要求」就這麼說

讀懂房屋廣告後，如何從中找出合適的住處呢？現在我們回頭看看閱讀租房廣告前高斌對住處的要求，把這些要求逐條寫下來，我們在閱讀廣告的時候，就可以很快判斷哪些住處比較適合他了。

✎ 寫出高斌對住處的要求。

rent (per week): _____

other requirements: _____

_____

✎ 寫下比較適合高斌的租屋廣告號碼。

Possible choice(s) for Gao Bin: _____

_____

提示與解析

rent (per week): £150—£175

other requirements:

a shared house or flat, near convenient bus stops, furnished, with cooking facilities, central heating, a fair rent

Possible choice(s) for Gao Bin: 3, 4

（這兩間的租金合適，而且都可以與人合租。第3條廣告的房子還離公車站很近，非常符合高斌的要求。）

別忘了，廣告中的資訊不見得完整，所以必要的話還是打電話去問！

十年英語不白學，「住處不合適的原因」就這麼說

　　在前一個練習中，我們發現第3條和第4條廣告中的住處很適合高斌。那其他住處為什麼不適合他呢？請用以下句型寫出句子，說明其他四個住處的問題。

The house / flat / room in Ad. x is not suitable for Gao Bin because ＿＿＿＿.

寫下這些住處不合適的原因。

1 Ad. 1

_____

_____

_____

2 Ad. 2

_____

_____

_____

3 Ad. 5

_____

_____

_____

4 Ad. 6

_____

_____

_____

提示與解析

參考答案：

❶ The flat in Ad. **1** is not suitable for Gao Bin because **it is too expensive and is for a single person or a couple.**

❷ The flat in Ad. **2** is not suitable for Gao Bin because **it is too expensive and not shared with other people.**

❸ The room in Ad. **5** is not suitable for Gao Bin because **there are no cooking facilities and students are preferred.**

❹ The bedsit in Ad. **6** is not suitable for Gao Bin because **there are no cooking facilities and females are preferred.**

拒當英文句點王，換你練習開口說說看！

看完解答後，請練習把這些句子大聲讀出來！

Part 2——
社交英語無師自通，
道地的「用電話詢問住處細節」該怎麼說？

十年英語不白學，「接通電話後」就這麼說

在前面的練習中，我們發現第3條與第4條租房廣告中的房子很適合高斌。於是，他先打了電話去問房東4號房的具體情況，但發現已經租給別人了。接下來，他又打電話問3號房的情況。想聽聽他與房東的對話嗎？請聽以下音檔。

聽一聽對話的開始部分，看一看以下的敘述，它們是正確的嗎？如果聽到「Yes, of course. Go ahead.」，請先把音檔暫停。

 在正確的敘述旁打勾。　　　◀️ *Track 001*

❶ The person making the call speaks first.
❷ The person answering the call speaks first.
❸ The person answering the call asks what the caller wants.
❹ The person answering the call simply states his / her name and / or telephone number.
❺ The person making the call states his / her business.
❻ The person making the call waits for the other person to ask him / her what he / she wants.

你覺得在電話中開始一個對話，用英文講和用中文講有什麼差別呢？把你想到的差別之處寫在下面。

_____

_____

_____

_____

提示與解析

正確的敘述是 ❷ , ❹ , ❺ 。

習慣講中文的人，和英文母語人士通電話時，要注意一些文化上的差異。中文在接電話的時候會說「喂」，英文母語人士則會說 "Hello"，但有時還會接著報上自己的名字、電話號碼、公司名稱等。像在這段會話中，接電話的人（房東先生）就說了 "Hello"，並報上自己的電話號碼3075219。接下來，打電話的人才會提出自己的問題或表明自己打電話的理由。舉例來說，在這段對話中，高斌說："I'm calling about the advertisement in the newspaper."（我打電話是要問報紙上租屋廣告的事情）。而其他人則有可能問："Is this Mary?"（是瑪麗嗎？）或 "Could I speak to Mary?"（可以請瑪麗來聽電話嗎？）

要注意英語國家與華人打電話習慣的差異，在英語國家，接電話的人會希望你開門見山地說明打電話的理由，而不是像華人習慣性地先講一些寒暄的話。

十年英語不白學，「詢問住處細節」就這麼說

　　打電話給房東前，高斌列了一個清單，記下他想問房東的資訊。因為他平常不是很習慣用英語打電話，他想先做好準備，所以在打電話前就先練習把所有問題讀出來。以下是他列的清單，讀一讀，想想看，如果你想了解這些資訊，會問哪些問題呢？

想了解這些資訊，該問什麼問題？

❶ sort of house

What sort of house is it?

❷ age of house

❸ size of house

_____

❹ other people living there

_____

❺ the facilities

_____

❻ the furniture

_____

❼ facilities in the area

_____

❽ distance from city centre

_____

❾ Chinese shops or restaurants nearby

_____

❿ phone bill included in rent or not

_____

⓫ the exact location

_____

提示與解析

參考答案：

❷ How old is the house?

❸ What size is the house? / How big is the house? / How many rooms does the house have?

❹ Are there any other people living in the house? / Who else lives in the house?

❺ What are the facilities in the house? / What facilities are there? / What are the facilities like?

6 What furniture is provided in the house? / What furniture is there?
7 What about the facilities in the local area? / What are the local facilities like?
8 Is the house far from the city centre / the place I work at? / How far is it from the city centre / the place I work at?
9 Are there any Chinese shops or restaurants nearby?
10 Is phone bill included in the rent?
11 What is the exact location of the house? / Where exactly is the house?

以上只是參考答案，你也可以寫下不一樣的句子。你可能會發現這些解答中經常用到這個句型：What is / are _____ like?（……是什麼樣子？）這個句型非常實用。

拒當英文句點王，換你練習開口說說看！

聽音檔中的對話，寫下高斌問的問題，並練習把這些問題讀出來。

🔊 聽音檔，根據括號中的提示寫出高斌問的關於房子的問題。
◀ *Track 001*

1 (sort of house)
_____

2 (furniture)
_____

3 (kitchen)
_____

4 (television)
_____

⑤ (telephone)

_____

⑥ (water, gas, electricity)

_____

⑦ (direct bus)

_____

⑧ (see the house)

_____

提示與解析

答案：

① What sort of house is it?
② Are the rooms fully furnished?
③ And what about the kitchen?
④ Is there a television in the house?
⑤ And what about a telephone?
⑥ Are water, gas and electricity included in the rent?
⑦ Is there a direct bus from the house?
⑧ Could I come and see the house this afternoon?

現在把高斌問的問題和我們在上一個練習中寫下的問題比較一下，是不是不太一樣呢？這是因為高斌在問問題的時候，多少會被對方所說的話影響。例如高斌會問："What about a telephone?"（那電話呢？），而不是問："Is there a telephone in the house?"（房子裡有電話嗎？），因為對方已經可以從對話中判斷他問的是房子的事，並且要問房子裡有哪些東西，所以高斌就不需要再重複問一次「房子裡有……嗎？」。語言使用真是很靈活吧。

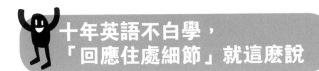

拒當英文句點王，換你練習開口說說看！
再次聽音檔，並重複高斌問的問題。◀Track 001

十年英語不白學，
「回應住處細節」就這麼說

聽完整段對話，記錄下和房子相關的資訊，完成以下表格。

🔊 聽音檔，完成表格。 ◀Track 001

sort of house	
size of house	
number of people sharing the house	
the furniture	
facilities in the kitchen	
facilities in the living room include...	
Chinese shops or restaurants nearby	
distance from Gao Bin's work place	
bus to the work place	
housing rent includes...	
phone bill included or not	
appointment time	

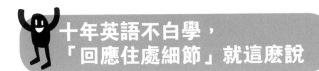

提示與解析

The house is a terraced house.

It has three floors with eight rooms.

Seven people share the house.

The rooms are furnished with a single bed, a wardrobe, a desk, a chair and a bookcase.

The kitchen has most cooking utensils except a Chinese wok.

The facilities in the living room include a TV set and a telephone.

There is a Chinese supermarket nearby.

The house is about half-an-hour walk from the place Gao Bin works at.

Gao Bin can take Bus 57 to his work place.

The housing rent includes water, gas and electricity bills.

The phone bill is not included in the rent.

Gao Bin is going to see the house at two o'clock in the afternoon.

Part 3——
社交英語無師自通，
道地的「社區內的各種設施」該怎麼說？

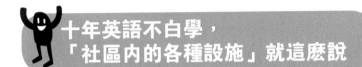

**十年英語不白學，
「社區內的各種設施」就這麼說**

　　在這個單元的開頭，我們討論了各種「居住場所」，當時也提到：無論住在哪裡，我們都一定住在 "community" 中。到底什麼是 "community" 呢？一個 "community" 指的是某個很多人共同居住或共同相處的區域。這裡先把它稱為「社區」，不過它和我們中文所說的「社區」比起來，範圍可以更大。在一個社區中，設施（facilities）非常重要，比如商店、銀行等。現在我們一起來想想看，一個社區中，到底該有哪些設施呢？

　　在住宅區，最基本的設施應該就是商店、市場。還有哪些呢？在下面寫出你居住的社區內及其附近的設施以及你覺得社區內應該增加的設施。我已經為你寫出了一些例子！

　　在橫線上寫出你居住的社區內及其附近的設施以及你覺得應該增加的設施。

facilities your community has: *post office, bank,* _____

_____

facilities that you think are also desirable: _____

_____

你寫下了哪些設施呢？這裡當然沒有固定的答案，下面列出了幾個你可能會想到的設施。接下來的練習中還會提到許許多多種不同的設施，可以對照看一看，你有沒有在這裡列出。

restaurant
supermarket
beauty salon
book store
telephone booth
park
library
news-stand
laundry
community centre

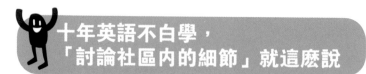

十年英語不白學，「討論社區內的細節」就這麼說

高斌和房東韋斯特先生（Mr. West）約了下午2點看房子，結果提早到了。他便趁這個時間在附近到處看看，並和路人聊了起來。

聽對話，寫下另一個說話者的名字，以及對話中提到的設施。

🔊 聽音檔，寫出以下資訊。　◀ *Track 002*

Gao Bin is talking to: _____

Who is the person? _____

The facilities mentioned in the conversation are: _____

_____

_____

提示與解析

- Gao Bin is talking to Jean Kingsley.
- She is a neighbour.
- The facilities mentioned in the conversation are:
  a park, a Chinese supermarket, a library, the community centre, a newsagent's, and a launderette

---

看看以下的敘述，再聽一遍對話，判斷這些語句是否正確，在正確的敘述前寫 T，不正確的敘述前寫 F。如果對話沒有提到相關資訊，則寫 N（No information）。我已經幫你做好第一題了！

🔊)) 聽音檔，做判斷。 ◀️ Track 002

(F) ❶ Gao Bin starts the conversation by commenting on the weather.

( ) ❷ Mrs. Kingsley starts the conversation by commenting on the house.

( ) ❸ The houses in the area are rather old.

( ) ❹ Mrs. Kingsley is a middle-aged woman.

( ) ❺ Mrs. Kingsley has lived in this area for thirty years.

( ) ❻ Mr. and Mrs. West lived in this area for almost forty years and moved to a smaller place a couple of years ago.

( ) ❼ Though Mr. and Mrs. West have moved out, their grandson still lives here.

( ) ❽ People living in this area get along with each other quite well.

( ) ❾ Mr. West's son often helps Mrs. Kingsley when she has problems.

(　) ⑩ Both young and old in this area often go to the park to enjoy themselves.

(　) ⑪ The local library not only provides people with newspapers, but also organises the delivery of newspapers to their houses.

(　) ⑫ The community centre provides the service of delivering newspapers to people's houses.

(　) ⑬ The newsagent's provides the service of delivering newspapers to people's houses.

(　) ⑭ There is a laundry as well as a launderette in the area.

(　) ⑮ Mrs. Kingsley doesn't think Gao Bin has much money and suggests he should go to the launderette.

(　) ⑯ Mrs. Kingsley suggests that Gao Bin go to the launderette since she thinks that young people can make friends there.

(　) ⑰ Gao Bin likes the place very much and hopes that Mr. West will accept him as a tenant.

(　) ⑱ Mrs. Kingsley has no idea whether Gao Bin will be accepted by Mr. West.

你能不能從上述的對話中了解到這個社區是否適合居住呢？為什麼？

_____

_____

_____ .

- 未提到（N）： ❸ , ❻ , ⓮

- 第4題：金斯利太太（Mrs. Kingsley）說她45年前結婚時搬到這一帶，可見她不可能是中年太太，應該至少有60多歲了。
- 第7題：還住在那棟房子裡的是韋斯特先生的兒子。
- 第9題：韋斯特先生以前會幫金斯利太太忙。
- 第11題和12題：圖書館和社區中心不提供送報紙服務。
- 第18題：金斯利太太認為韋斯特先生會租房子給高斌。

對了，你知道對話中的 "laundry" 和 "launderette" 有什麼區別嗎？原來，要請人幫你洗衣服的時候，應該拿去 "laundry"。而在 "launderette"，不會有人幫你洗衣服，它只提供洗衣機和烘衣機，你可以自己洗。這些機器通常是投幣式的（coin-operated），直接將錢投入投幣口（slot）就行。

我們可以猜測，這個區域應該是適合居住的，首先感覺居民比較友善，而且設施比較完善。此外，金斯利太太還說她已經在這裡住了40多年，完全沒有想過搬到別的地方去住。

十年英語不白學，「想延續對話」就這麼說

你注意到這段對話中使用的問句了嗎？金斯利太太一開始就說："Are you looking at the house? Nice, isn't it?" 聊到公園時，她又說："OK, the park is lovely, isn't it?" 後來在談到洗衣服很貴時，還說："You're not made of money, are you?"

對話中，"isn't it?" 和 "are you?" 這類問句，用途是什麼呢？其實是想和別人確認他們的想法，並將對話繼續下去，並不是真的想要對方詳細回答問題。大多數人和陌生人或不熟的人對話時，經常會使用這種問句。這裡金斯利太太也一樣，為了和高斌將聊天繼續下去，使用了這些簡短的問句。以下有幾個這種簡短問句的示例，都是用來開啟話題的。請將問句和下面表格中的各種情境搭配在一起。

把下面的問句和表格中相應的情境搭配在一起。

a. They're cheap, aren't they?　　b. They're not cheap, are they?
c. The service is very slow, isn't it?　d. This is a lovely place, isn't it?
e. It's very stuffy in here, isn't it?　f. It's already fifteen minutes late, isn't it?
g. Dreadful weather, isn't it?　　h. The strawberries look good, don't they?

❶ sitting beside a river	d
❷ waiting long for a coach at the coach station	
❸ waiting for a bus in the rain	
❹ waiting for the waitress in a restaurant	
❺ standing at a fruit stall	
❻ looking at some very low-priced videos	
❼ buying expensive tickets to go into a museum	
❽ sitting in a very hot waiting room on a summer day	

提示與解析

❷ f ❸ g ❹ c ❺ h ❻ a ❼ b ❽ e

仔細看一看這些問句與陳述部分的搭配。「肯定」的陳述部分一般會搭配「否定」的問句，而「否定」的陳述部分一般則會搭配「肯定」的問句。問句和陳述部分的主詞要一致，並使用代名詞取代名詞主詞。

拒當英文句點王，換你練習開口說說看！

練習讀一讀上頁中表格上方的句子吧！

十年英語不白學，「想在特定場合中和陌生人聊天」就這麼說

　　在許多情況下，擅自跑去和陌生人搭訕是不合適的。但在某些情境下，如排隊等候公車、看電影或話劇間隙時等，和陌生人聊天是可以接受的。

　　想像一下，在以下這些情境中，你會如何開始和旁邊的陌生人聊天呢？

用反意疑問句寫出你在各個情境下可能會說的話。

❶ You are in a very slow queue / line-up at a supermarket.

You could say: _____

❷ It's the interval during a very amusing play in the theatre.

You could say: _____

❸ You are in a flower shop where there are some very nice roses.

You could say: _____

❹ An elder lady sits down beside you on a bench in a quiet park.

You could say: _____

❺ You are in a very crowded waiting room at the railway station.

You could say: _____

⑥ You feel bored waiting for the machine to finish washing your clothes at the launderette.

You could say: _____

❼ You are talking to another customer at the hairdresser's, about a very modern hairstyle in a magazine.

You could say: _____

⑧ You notice a group of children playing happily in the park.

You could say: _____

提示與解析

我為各種情境都提供了兩個可能的答案。以下這些都是供參考的說法，你也可以有一些其他不同的答案，不過，無論你的答案是什麼都一定要注意句子前後部分主詞一致，而且在「肯定的敘述」後面一般要加上「否定的問句」，在「否定的敘述」後一般要加上「肯定的問句」。

參考答案：
① This is taking a long time, isn't it? / It's not exactly quick, is it?
② It's very funny, isn't it? / The actors are great, aren't they?
③ The roses are really lovely, aren't they? / The roses look beautiful, don't they?
④ It's a lovely day, isn't it? / It's lovely and quiet, isn't it?
⑤ It's crowded today, isn't it? / There are lots of people, aren't there?
⑥ It's boring, isn't it? / It takes a long time, doesn't it?
❼ It's lovely, isn't it? / It's very fashionable, isn't it?
⑧ They're really sweet, aren't they? / They seem happy, don't they?

Part 4—
社交英語無師自通，
道地的「各種設施的功用」該怎麼說？

**十年英語不白學，
「社區內各種場所、設施的功用」就這麼說**

　　韋斯特先生很開心地把其中一間房間租給高斌了。高斌搬進了新家，非常期待好好了解一下他所居住的社區，好讓生活步入正軌。他寫了一張清單，列出所有自己需要做的事，而且他知道在做這些事情的過程中，他就會開始漸漸融入這裡的生活了。以下是高斌列的清單。他要去哪些地方才能完成這些事呢？把需要的地點名稱寫在清單每一項前面的括號中，並用以下的句型，仿照範例造句。最後還可以練習讀一讀整個句子！

　　寫下高斌完成需要做的事情的地點並寫出完整的句子。

❶ (　　　　　　　) — organise finances / get a cheque book or credit card

❷ (　　　　　　　) — borrow some books about the area

❸ (　　　　　　　) — buy stamps and post letters back home

❹ (　　　　　　　) — order newspapers to be delivered to the house

❺ (　　　　　　　) — have shoes repaired

❻ (　　　　　　　) — have a haircut

❼ (　　　　　　　) — have films (of London photographs) developed

❽ (　　　　　　　) — get a discount bus card

答案:

❶ Gao Bin needs to go to the bank to organise his finances or to get a cheque book or credit card.

❷ He needs to go to a library to borrow some books.

❸ He needs to go to the post office to buy stamps and post letters back home.

❹ He needs to go to the newsagent's to order newspapers to be delivered to the house.

❺ He needs to go to the shoe-repairer's (or cobbler's) to have his shoes repaired.

❻ He needs to go to a hairdresser's (or barber's) to have a haircut.

❼ He needs to go to a photographer's (or a film-developer's) to have his films developed.

❽ He needs to go to the bus terminal (or bus station) to get a discount bus card.

拒當英文句點王,換你練習開口說說看!

寫完句子後,練習讀一讀整個句子,讓你的英語口語更流利!例如:

(police station) —to get registered
You say: *He needs to go to the police station to get registered.*

十年英語不白學, 「場所、設施的相關事項」就這麼說

下面方框中的所有單字或片語都和當地社區的設施相關。想想看,在表格中的不同地點會使用到哪些單字或片語呢?把相關的單字或片語填入表格中適當的位置。我已經為你完成一些例子了!

將以下方框中的單字或片語填入表格適當的位置。

account	airmail sticker	spin dryer	hairdryer	negative	tumble dryer
heel	on loan	cheque	trim	enlargement	say "cheese"	post card
sole	perm	overdraft	detergent	interest rate	leather	stylist
special delivery	lace	shave	washer	postage	author index	registered
shampoo and set	subject catalogue	washing powder	laundry bag
washing cycle	developed and printed	appointment	processing time
washing machine	

Local facilities	Commonly used words or phrases
Bank	account　　cheque　　overdraft　　interest rate
Post office	
Hairdresser's	
Launderette	
Photographer's	
Shoe repairer's	
Library	

答案：

Post office: airmail sticker, post card, special delivery, postage, registered

Hairdresser's: hairdryer, trim, perm, stylist, shampoo and set, shave, appointment

Launderette: spin dryer, tumble dryer, detergent, washer, washing powder, laundry bag, washing cycle, washing machine

Photographer's: negative, enlargement, say "cheese", developed and printed, processing time

Shoe repairer's: heel, sole, leather, lace

Library: on loan, author index, subject catalogue

十年英語不白學，
「場所、設施內的對話」就這麼說

　　閱讀下面幾段簡短的對話，想想看，這些對話可能是在哪裡發生的。將地點寫在各段對話前面的括號中。如果對話可以發生在多個場所，就在括號中寫下 "general"（概括「多個地方」）。

 寫出以下對話最可能發生的地點。

❶ (　　　　　) A: You booked for a perm, didn't you?
　　　　　　　　B: Yes, but I'd like it cut as well, please.

❷ (　　　　　) A: How many prints would you like?
　　　　　　　　B: I'd like two ordinary prints from these negatives and two enlargements from these.

3 (   )   A: May I ask your opening hours?
                        B: From 9 a.m. to 5 p.m.

4 (   )   A: Could you weigh this letter for me?
                        B: It's over 10 grams.

5 (   )   A: Is it possible to borrow this book for another week?
                        B: Just one moment. I'll have to check whether anyone wants
                            to borrow it.

6 (   )   A: Would you fill in this form, please?
                        B: Yes, of course.

7 (   )   A: How would you like it, sir?
                        B: Just give it a good trim, please. I like this style but it's a
                            bit too long.

8 (   )   A: How would you like to send it? Registered or just ordinary?
                        B: I think it should be registered. It contains my passport.

9 (   )   A: Special cleaning or ordinary cleaning?
                        B: I think the ordinary will be fine, thank you.

10 (   )   A: Can you give me some help finding a book please?
                        B: Well, it's very easy. They are all arranged by subject, in
                            alphabetical order.

11 (   )   A: What coins do I need for the washing machines and
                            dryers?
                        B: The washers take pound coins; the dryers use 20 or 50
                            pence.

12 (   )   A: Could you let me have some extra airmail stickers,
                            please? I use rather a lot of them.
                        B: Certainly. These should last you a few weeks.

⑬ (　　　　) A: I'd like these shoes soled, please.
B: Leather or rubber?

⑭ (　　　　) A: I'd like to deposit this cheque, please.
B: Ah! You'll need to complete this paying-in slip first.

提示與解析

答案：

① a hairdresser's
② a photographer's
③ general
④ a post office
⑤ a library
⑥ general
⑦ a hairdresser's
⑧ a post office
⑨ a dry cleaner's
⑩ a library
⑪ a launderette
⑫ a post office
⑬ a shoe repairer's
⑭ a bank

十年英語不白學，「其他場所、設施內可進行的活動」就這麼說

我們現在已經學習了許多人們在日常生活中會使用的設施的名稱。當然，還有很多場所、都是大家平常會去的，如：

clinic（診所）
restaurant（餐廳）
cinema（電影院）
video rental store（影片出租店）

tailor's（裁縫店）
playground（遊樂場）
…

社交英語無師自通，你一定還想知道更多！

現在請你想像一下，當對方有某種特定需求時，你該如何給他建議？請用下面這個句型來提出建議：

If you want..., you should go to..., which is...

有些事情我們可以自己做（**do for ourselves**），有些事情必須請別人幫我們做（**have sth. done for us**）。在練習說這些句子的時候，要記得選擇正確的形式！看下面的兩句例句，了解兩者的差別：

If you want to develop your films...（如果你想要洗照片⋯⋯）

If you want to have your films developed...（如果你想請人幫你洗照片⋯⋯）

 請根據下列需求，提出建議。

❶ rent video tapes / the place is next to the supermarket

You say: *If you want to rent some video tapes, you should go to the video rental shop, which is next to the supermarket.*

❷ send a parcel / the place is opposite the bank

❸ make a new suit / the place is on the corner of Laurel Road

❹ check your teeth / the place is on the left, just before you get to the park

❺ take your photograph / the place is next to the library

❻ deliver your newspapers / the place is next to the bank

❼ dry clean your winter coat / the place is opposite the post office

❽ dye you hair / the place is upstairs from the supermarket

提示與解析

答案：

2 If you want to send a parcel, you should go to the post office, which is opposite the bank.

3 If you want to have a new suit made, you should go to the tailor's, which is on the corner of Laurel Road.

4 If you want to have your teeth checked, you should go to the clinic, which is on the left, just before you get to the park.

5 If you want to have your photograph taken, you should go to the photographer's, which is next to the library.

6 If you want to have your newspapers delivered, you should go to the newsagent's, which is next to the bank.

7 If you want to have your winter coat dry cleaned, you should go to the dry cleaner's, which is opposite the post office.

8 If you want to have your hair dyed, you should go to the hairdresser's, which is upstairs from the supermarket.

你都答對了嗎？希望你已經都掌握了！

Part 5——
社交英語無師自通，
道地的「社區安全計劃」該怎麼說？

十年英語不白學，
「社區安全計劃的相關事項」就這麼說

　　高斌正在警局登記，順便問了警察幾個關於安全的問題。他從朋友那裡聽說，在曼徹斯特還是容易發生盜竊案的。警察告訴他，這裡有個叫做 "Neighbourhood Watch" 的社區安全計劃，能夠幫助降低犯罪率，警察還順便拿了一張單子給他參考。高斌這才想起，他剛搬進的房子窗戶上就貼著一張寫著 "Neighbourhood Watch" 的宣傳單。你將要讀到的 Text 1 是單子上列出的一些資訊。其中每項資訊的標題都被移到下面的方框中了，請把這些標題放回正確的位置（標●處）吧！

閱讀宣傳單，把正確的標題放到下頁Text 1適當的地方。

- **Things you need to report**

- **Aims of Neighbourhood Watch schemes**

- **Information the police will need**

- **Advantages of the schemes**

- **Working staff of the schemes**

NEIGHBOURHOOD WATCH
A guide to community action against crime

Wherever you live, you are part of a community. It may be large or small, in a town or in the country. It might be a housing estate, a rural village, a block of flats, a suburban road or a seaside resort. Unfortunately, regardless of its size your community may be a likely target for the criminal.

It is easy to shrug it off and assume that it won't happen to you or that nothing can be done. In fact, a great deal can be done to prevent crime. But the police cannot do it alone. Each of us has a vital role to play by becoming actively involved in crime prevention.

● ❶
— to reduce local opportunities for crime thereby deterring would-be thieves and vandals;
— to establish a community spirit so that everyone can contribute towards the protection of their property by mutual co-operation and communication;
— to inform the coordinator or the police of any suspicious activity.

● ❷
— the results of Neighbourhood Watch schemes already established show that they can help to reduce local crime such as burglaries, vandalism, car thefts and thefts from cars;
— a better community spirit can be created; suspicious strangers waiting outside schools, in parks and playgrounds where children congregate, can be quickly reported to the police;
— crime prevention advice can be quickly and efficiently circulated throughout the community.

●

Only with the support of the majority of residents, can Neighbourhood Watch operate successfully. Most schemes have one or more coordinators. These are people who normally spend long periods at home, and who receive information from other residents about anything suspicious they may have seen or heard, and then pass it on to the police.

Neighbourhood Watch schemes lead to a greater shared awareness of the problems in your community and to a better understanding of the practical steps that can be taken to tackle these.

●

By being a good neighbour, and keeping an eye out for anything suspicious you can help to make your community more secure. Please report the police when you see:
— strangers knocking on front doors or peering through windows then disappearing round the back, or loitering suspiciously;
— strangers hanging round schools, playing fields, etc., and approaching children;
— open windows in houses where the owners are out or on holidays;
— strangers trying car doors;
— anything that you believe is suspicious.

● ⑤

— an exact description of what you have seen;
— the time;
— the place;
— the person(s) involved: approximate age, sex, height, build, unusual characteristics, clothing worn, and any other distinguishing features;
— the vehicles involved: registration number (even part of this number might help), make and model (if known), colour and direction of travel.

答案：

1 Aims of Neighbourhood Watch schemes

2 Advantages of the schemes

3 Working staff of the schemes

4 Things you need to report

5 Information the police will need

十年英語不白學，
「社區安全計劃的摘要」就這麼說

　　下面是 "Neighbourhood Watch" 的摘要，其中有一些單字被拿掉了，變成了空格。請從下面的方框中選擇適當的單字填入空格中。如果需要，可以將整段文字再讀一遍。

　利用方框中的單字完成摘要。

schemes	*vandalism*	*thefts*
community	*crime*	*responsible*
neighbourhood	*members*	*prevent*
police	*coordinator*	*active*
contact	*notice*	*operation*

Anyone, in any (1) _____, can be the victim of (2) _____, so it is important for everyone to help the police (3) _____ crime. Neighbourhood Watch (4) _____ operate in several communities. Each scheme has at least one local (5) _____ who is in charge of his / her area and (6) _____ for keeping the (7) _____ informed of what is happening in the (8) _____. Members of the scheme who (9) _____ anything suspicious can either (10) _____ the coordinator or talk directly to the police. Crime figures in areas where these schemes are now in (11) _____ indicate that local crimes such as burglaries, (12) _____, car thefts and (13) _____ from cars can be reduced when (14) _____ of the community take an (15) _____ role in crime prevention.

提示與解析

答案：

1. community 2. crime 　3. prevent 　　4. schemes 　5. coordinator
6. responsible 7. police 　8. neighbourhood 9. notice 　　10. contact
11. operation 12. vandalism 13. thefts 　　14. members 15. active

---

　　下頁方框中的單字或片語都出現在 Text 1 中，請把它們找出來，並根據上下文猜猜它們的意思。接下來，依據自己猜測的意思，把這些單字或片語填入方框下方的句子中。

請使用方框中的單字或片語完成句子。

shrug... off	become involved in	deter from	hang around
circulate	tackle	loiter	approach	congregate
contribute to / towards			

❶ You can easily _____ keeping your own building tidy by taking care of your own rubbish.

❷ Many communities have their own newspapers and these newspapers generally sell well, because they are one of the chief ways to _____ local news, good or bad.

❸ People generally _____ in this main square on Sundays and public holidays—to chat to each other, have a drink together and to watch what's going on!

❹ If you are lost, it is wise to _____ a policeman and ask for directions.

❺ Though people understand the problems of water shortage, when the government calls on them to economise on water, most of them simply _____ it _____.

❻ There is so much crime in the area that teenagers are advised not to _____ chatting to their friends in public places after dark.

❼ A good way of getting to know your community is to _____ all kinds of local activities by joining clubs, the community centre and so on.

❽ It's unwise to _____ in public places. It makes people suspicious.

❾ The local police sometimes find it difficult to _____ the problem of domestic arguments and family problems.

❿ Big dogs in houses often _____ burglars from breaking in.

提示與解析

答案：

1 contribute to / towards　　2 circulate　　3 congregate
4 approach　　5 shrug... off　　6 hang around
7 become involved in　　8 loiter　　9 tackle
10 deter

"loiter" 和 "hang around" 的意思非常相近，都表示「在某處閒逛」，但差別
是："loiter" 指的是漫無目的地在某處閒逛，令人覺得很可疑，會讓人猜測他
到底在這裡做什麼。而 "hang around" 指的同樣是在某處閒逛，但不會令人覺
得可疑。此外，還有個特別的單字 "congregate"，"congregate" 是「集合」
的意思，但並不是毫無目的地集合，而是「有目的」地集合。

十年英語不白學，「各項設施的宣傳」就這麼說

　　高斌收集了許多單子，上面提供了不少關於這一帶的資訊，種類繁多。這些
單子通常都是免費領取的，很實用。他在圖書館拿到一張單子，上面提供了關於
社區中心的資訊，而且社區中心正好就在高斌的新家旁邊。54頁的Text 2 列出了
這張單子上提供的資訊，如果看到不認識的單字，可以先根據上下文猜測意思，
如果猜不出來，可以翻開辭典查查看。

　　高斌喜歡各種不同的運動，他也喜歡集郵，但不喜歡玩牌及棋盤遊戲。閱讀
54頁的Text 2，結合上述資訊，回答下列問題。

閱讀54頁的 **Text 2** 中提供的資訊，回答以下問題。

❶ Does the Laurel Tempest Centre provide any special sports facilities? ___

If "Yes", write down the special facilities provided:

_____

If "No", where should Gao Bin go?

He should go to _____.

❷ Is there a club or society in the Centre that Gao Bin could join in to satisfy his interest in stamp collecting? _____

If "Yes", write the name of the club or society here: _____

If "No", where can he seek information from? He can phone or go to ___.

❸ How much would Gao Bin have to pay to join the community centre? ___

❹ Does the membership fee include the costs of all clubs and classes? ___

❺ Who is Dave Hamilton? _____

❻ We can be certain that some of the clubs or societies will be of no interest to Gao Bin. Which are they? (You need not write the reasons but you should think about them!)

_____

_____

❼ Which clubs or societies may be of interest to Gao Bin?

_____

❽ Are refreshments provided free of charge? _____

❾ What does GDCS stand for? _____

⑩ What do you think the warden's job is?

_____

⑪ If Gao Bin wants to find out the time of the clubs or societies that he's interested in, what should he do?

_____

⑫ If Gao Bin decides to join the community centre, what does he need to do?

_____

DISTRICT COUNCIL
COMMUNITY SERVICES
RECREATION AND AMENITIES

LAUREL TEMPEST CENTRE
Laurel Road, Gilmore
Tel. 3077831

The Laurel Tempest Centre is a division of Gilmore District Community Services. The main special sports facilities are located in the Gilmore Sports Centre. The Laurel Tempest Centre offers a range of facilities for YOU and your community. A year's membership to the centre entitles you to make use of these facilities and gives you the opportunity to mix with other members of the community.

GENERAL MEMBERSHIP FEE (for 12 months):
standard: £12
unwaged, over 60's, students: £6

Membership forms can be obtained from the Gilmore Sports Centre or the Laurel Tempest Centre. Completed forms, together with the membership fee should be handed to Dave Hamilton, at the centre, between 9 a.m. and 5 p.m. on weekdays.

Please note: individual clubs / groups at the centre may also charge a small fee to cover running costs, etc.

LAUREL TEMPEST ACTIVITIES

Toddler Group　　Over Sixties Club　　　Chess Club　　Bridge Club
Karate Classes　　　Dog Training Classes　　Local History Society
Bowling Club　　　Philatelist Society　　　Photography Club
Under Fives Ballet Classes　　　Women's Self-defense Classes

Details of all the above activities or other information can be obtained, by phone or in person, from the Laurel Tempest office.

The Refreshment Room serves mid-priced tea, coffee and home-made snacks between 10 a.m. and 11 a.m. every day (except Sunday) and between 2 p.m. and 3 p.m. on Saturdays.

The rooms in the centre can be booked for regular meetings or occasional functions. For details, please contact the warden, Dave Hamilton, or telephone 3077831.

GDCS WORKING FOR YOU GDCS WORKING FOR YOU

提示與解析

答案：
1. No. He should go to the Gilmore Sports Centre.
2. Yes. The Philatelist Society. (「集郵」的英文專業說法是 "philately"。)
3. £12. (高斌不是學生，有工作，也不超過60歲。)
4. No. (有些俱樂部會收一點費用)
5. The warden.

⑥ Toddler Group, Over Sixties Club, Chess Club, Bridge Club, Dog Training Classes, Under Fives Ballet Classes and Women's Self-defense Classes.

⑦ As well as the Philatelist Society, he may be interested in the Photography Club, the Local History Society and, perhaps, the Karate Classes.

⑧ No.（它們比較便宜，即mid-priced）

⑨ Gilmore District Community Services.

⑩ The warden's job includes collecting completed membership forms, taking care of the building and the administration of the centre.

⑪ He should telephone the office of the centre.

⑫ He should collect an application form from the Laurel Tempest Centre or the Gilmore Sports Centre, fill it in, and take it to the warden between 9 a.m. and 5 p.m. on a weekday, together with the £12 membership fee.

社交英語無師自通，你一定還想知道更多！

　　你知道為什麼這裡用了 "unwaged"（無薪）這個單字嗎？為什麼不用比較常見的 "unemployed"（無業）呢？原來，"unwaged" 是個相對禮貌的說法，也就是說，不會冒犯他人。有些人雖然沒有領薪水，但他們一樣還是在工作，例如做慈善事業、在教會或社區工作，再比如說，家庭主婦也是一種工作，但她們沒有薪水可拿。正因為如此，這張傳單上才會使用 "unwaged" 這個比較不會冒犯他人的說法。

Part 6——
社交英語無師自通，道地的「處理銀行事務」該怎麼說？

　　你有銀行帳戶嗎？如果你每月領工資，你是拿現金、拿支票還是銀行會固定為你入帳呢？過去許多人都是領取現金，但是現在正在逐漸改變。比如在英國，有些人是以 "standing order" 的方式領薪水的。"standing order" 的意思就是說，這些人工作的公司會安排每個月的固定時間將薪水存入他們的銀行帳戶中。還有些人是領支票（cheques），他們必須自己拿支票去銀行存入帳戶。這裡的主角高斌就屬於後者，公司每個月會發給他支票。既然要能夠使用支票，他就需要辦一個銀行帳戶。

十年英語不白學，「各種不同的銀行帳户」就這麼說

　　高斌到了銀行，就問諮詢櫃臺的工作人員各種帳戶有哪些差別。工作人員向他大概說明後又給了他一張單子，也就是以下的 Text 3，請他回家自己慢慢研究。現在請你快速看一遍這張單子，記下其中提到的銀行帳戶種類吧！

閱讀以下單子，記下其中提到的銀行帳户種類。

The accounts described in the leaflet are:

ⓐ_____

ⓑ_____

ⓒ_____

Text 3

A Quick Guide to
Tinlays Bank Accounts

Tinlays Bank has more than sixty years experience of looking after other people's money. Whether you have fortunes or a few pounds, you can be sure we will take excellent care of them for you.

With branches and cashpoint machines all over the country, in small villages as well as major cities, we are there whenever you need us. Our staff are always willing to offer expert advice and answer any queries you may have.

This leaflet describes the major types of accounts you can open with us but we provide all sorts of other financial services too. Pop into your local branch for further details.

TINLAYS SAVINGS ACCOUNT: if you do not need regular access to your money, you can arrange to open a savings account. You can start a savings account with only £20 and add to it as often as you wish. Your money will earn you interest so your money will grow as you save. Interest rates vary depending on how much money you have in your account and whether you elect to leave it untouched for periods of three months, six months, one year, five years and so on. If, by any chance, you need access to your money at other times, you can make special arrangements with the bank. Our staff will be only too happy to advise you on the most profitable arrangement for your situation.

TINLAYS HIGHER RATE DEPOSIT ACCOUNT: If you wish to deposit sums in excess of £1,000 for a fixed period (minimum one year), our Higher Rate Deposit Account is for you. Attractive interest rates apply. Rates vary according to the sum you deposit. Ask for details at our personal banking desk.

TINLAYS CURRENT ACCOUNT: You can open a current account with as little as £1. You can deposit money, cash or cheques, as often as you wish. You will be issued with a personalised cheque book and a cash card. You can withdraw money with your cash card at any of our cashpoint machines, as often as you wish, as long as there are adequate funds in your account. As long as you stay in credit, there are no bank charges. Overdraft facilities are available by special arrangement. We provide special services for students and teenage account holders.

Choose the account(s) to suit your personal requirements. You may open just one type of account, two accounts, or even all three! Just fill in the appropriate application form(s) and present it / them to one of the personal bankers in any branch of TINLAYS.

TINLAYS APPLICATION FORMS ARE AVAILABLE AT ALL TINLAYS BRANCHES.

我相信要找到各種不同的帳戶應該不難吧！一共有三種：(1) savings account；
(2) higher rate deposit account； (3) current account。

　　高斌相信，他的月薪應該夠他生活了，而且運氣好的話還能存一點錢，多買點東西，甚至在回國前可以去度個假。然而，現在高斌還沒辦法考慮那麼遠，他最需要的還是能確保有應急用的錢，畢竟他目前也還搞不清楚在英國生活一周究竟要花多少錢。而且，他也希望能夠在採購比較貴的物品時，可以寫支票，而不用帶大量現金在身上。他聽說大部分西方人在付房租、付水電費、餐館用餐、商店購物時，都不付現金，而是寫支票或用信用卡。現在請大家看一看 Text 3 裡面提到的銀行帳戶種類，為高斌選擇最適合的一種吧！

為高斌選擇最適合他的帳戶種類。

The best account for Gao Bin is _____

If he opens this type of account, he will be given: _____

_____

高斌希望能夠隨時提錢，因此最適合他的帳戶種類應該是 "current account"。另外兩種帳戶都只允許他在特定的時間、經過特別的安排才能提錢。如果他開了一個 "current account"，銀行就會給他一本 "personalised cheque book"（個人支票本）和一張 "cash card"（現金提款卡）。

十年英語不白學，
「想了解銀行帳户的小細節」就這麼說

讀一讀前面的 Text 3，找出銀行帳户的小細節，回答以下問題。

閱讀並回答問題。

❶ Gao Bin knows that he needs to go to other cities or towns on business now and then. Why is it sensible for him to open an account with Tinlays bank rather than a smaller, more personal bank?

_____

❷ The interest rate of the Tinlays Higher Rate Deposit Account is indeed very attractive to Gao Bin, yet he knows that he cannot open one. What is / are the reason(s)?

_____

❸ Is it possible for one to withdraw some money when the bank is closed? If so, how?

_____

❹ Gao Bin has heard that it is only possible to withdraw money from a current account every three days. Is this information correct? If not, how frequently can a person withdraw money?

_____

❺ Money can be withdrawn from an account on the condition that:

_____

❻ The bank does not charge anything for administering the account on the condition that:

_____

提示與解析

參考答案：

❶ Tinlays bank has branches and automated teller machines all over the country.

❷ Large sums of money (in excess of £1,000) must be deposited for periods of more than one year. Gao Bin needs to get his money regularly. He doesn't have a lot of spare money and he will only be in Britain for six months.

❸ Yes, from a cashpoint machine. These machines are located outside banks. You have a special card which you insert in the machine and a special number which you "tap into" the machine, and then you can withdraw money immediately.

❹ No. People can withdraw money as often as he / she chooses.

❺ There are adequate funds (i.e. enough money) in your account.

❻ You stay / Your account stays in credit (i.e. as long as you do not spend more money than you have in your account by writing too many cheques etc.).

在 Text 3 中，找出以下方框中的單字和片語，並以畫底線的方式標出。如果有不認識的單字或片語，可以根據上下文，猜猜它們的意思。大概推敲出來後，就從這些單字或片語中挑選最合適的填寫在下頁的句子中。把單字或片語填入最適當的地方即可，不用每個都使用。

 從方框中選擇單字或片語完成以下句子。

account	cashpoint machine	savings account	interest
interest rate	deposit	cash	cheque
deposit account	current account	cheque book	cash card
withdraw	funds	in credit	bank charges
overdraft			

1 When you put money into the bank, you _____ it.

2 When you take money out of the bank, you _____ it.

3 So long as you have money in your account, you are _____.

4 The costs that you sometimes have to pay the bank for its services are called _____.

5 The extra money that you receive if you leave a sum of money in the bank for a particular period of time is called _____.

6 The sort of account you open in a bank that you can add money to at any time but not withdraw it at any time is a(n) _____.

7 The sort of account which allows you to deposit and withdraw money at any time is called a(n) _____.

8 The machine from which you can withdraw money is called a(n) _____.

9 The card you use to withdraw money from a machine is called a(n) _____.

10 An arrangement with a bank that allows you to spend more money than you have in your account (in other words, the arrangement which allows you to borrow the bank's money) is called a(n) _____.

提示與解析

答案：
❶ deposit　　❷ withdraw　　❸ in credit　　❹ bank charges
❺ interest　　❻ savings account　　❼ current account　　❽ cashpoint machine
❾ cash card　❿ overdraft

Part 7——
社交英語無師自通，
道地的「初來乍到遇到的情況」該怎麼說？

十年英語不白學，
「初來乍到遇到的情況」就這麼說

　　或許你一輩子都不會搬去國外，住在國外的社區，但你還是有可能在自家的社區遇到搬過來住的外國人，需要你幫助他們了解當地事務。相信你現在已經能夠比較有自信地使用英文和別人討論社區相關的事情了吧。你對非中式的社區應該也越來越了解了，對不對？那麼，遇到以下這些情況，你會怎麼說，怎麼做呢？

選出最恰當的選項。

❶ When dealing with people who work in libraries, post offices, banks,
　　a. it's essential to be polite and call them sir or madam.
　　b. it's necessary to be polite but you need not address them as sir or madam.

❷ When you need information from somewhere,
　　a. you always need an appointment.
　　b. you can usually ask the staff.

❸ Information leaflets are usually provided
　　a. free of charge.
　　b. for a modest charge.

❹ When you meet adults for the first time, you should address them
　　a. by their first name plus family name.
　　b. just by their family name.
　　c. by their family name plus title.

⑤ If you were introducing Jean Kingsley to your friend's ten-year-old son, you would introduce her as

a. Mrs. Kingsley.

b. grandma.

c. Auntie Jean.

⑥ When making a phone call, you

a. keep on saying "hello" until the person receiving the call asks what you want.

b. wait for the person who answers to speak, and then state what you want.

提示與解析

答案：❶ b ❷ b ❸ a ❹ c ❺ a ❻ b

Part 8——
社交英語無師自通，
道地的「描述我的新家」該怎麼寫？

　　你現在已經完成這一單元所有的活動了！請你再復習一遍全部的內容，如果有什麼不懂的地方，一定要找老師或朋友問清楚。

學完這一單元，你就可以：

☐ 詢問並找到附近的設施。

☐ 描述附近設施。

☐ 透過手冊或傳單獲取資訊。

☐ 閱讀並回覆租屋廣告。

☐ 討論租屋相關事項。

☐ 與鄰居閒聊。

☐ 看懂銀行理財方面的指示。

　　下頁的 Text 4 是從一封信件中摘取出來的，內容是一名英國學生向朋友描述自己的新家。參考這段文字，想像一下，如果你是高斌，想用英文寫兩段文字向朋友描述自己的新家，你會怎麼寫呢？你可以回顧本單元前面的內容，弄清楚高斌的家到底是什麼樣子。

Text 4

I was lucky enough to find a very nice place to live in soon after I arrived. The rent's only £150 a week, plus my share of the bills. It's a room in a flat in a high-rise block. There are three other tenants and though we each have our own rooms, we share the sitting room, kitchen and bathroom. The rooms are quite well furnished and there's everything I need in the kitchen—except a coffee machine (but, fortunately, I can borrow one from a friend). There's a television in the sitting room but no telephone. That should save me quite a bit of money. I'll have to get used to writing letters instead! I haven't yet spent much time with the other tenants but I don't foresee any problems.

The block is in rather a rough neighbourhood but our next-door neighbour seems a nice guy. He's rather quiet but very helpful. He's already told me where to find the best pubs and so on. There are a few shops nearby so I can do most of my shopping locally, but I'll have to go into town for most other things. It's only about a twenty-minute walk from the town centre, which is just as well since the buses don't seem to run very often!

寫下兩段文字描述高斌的新家。題目為 "My New Home"。

請使用以下標題：

<u>My New Home</u>

第一單元總復習

十年英語不白學，「想幫忙新鄰居了解新環境時」就這麼說

尼爾・赫德森（Neil Hudson）剛搬進了新家，他正在詢問鄰居附近社區有哪些設施。 ◀ *Track 003*

聽聽他們的對話，回答下面尼爾想了解的問題。

Rubbish collection—when?	
Stair cleaners—when & how much?	
Nearest dry cleaner's?	
Nearest post office?	
Drying clothes?	
Anything else?	

提示與解析

Rubbish collection—when?	Mondays & Thursdays, 7 a.m.—put the bin on the pavement the night before
Stair cleaners—when & how much?	Fridays—£1.50 a week—give money to neighbour
Nearest dry cleaner's?	Down the street on the left, about two blocks down—open to 8 p.m.

Nearest post office?	Right, 100 yards, across the road
Drying clothes?	Communal garden—look for the key to back door
Anything else?	Gardener—£5 a month—1st Saturday each month

MP3音檔內容完整看

　　若是聽完音檔還是没把握，建議可搭配本部份學習，不熟的語彙要查辭典並作筆記，方能加深英文記憶。

Part 2: Track 001 （請配合022、025、027頁及音檔使用）

Mr. West: Hello. 3075219.

Gao Bin: Hello. I'm calling about the advertisement in the newspaper. Are the rooms still available?

Mr. West: Yes, they are. Would you like to make an appointment to come and see them?

Gao Bin: Well, could I ask you a few questions first?

Mr. West: Yes, of course. Go ahead.

Gao Bin: What sort of house is it?

Mr. West: Well, it's a terraced house with three floors and eight rooms all together. I usually have seven people living here, sharing the kitchen and bathroom.

Gao Bin: Are the rooms fully furnished? You see, I'll only be here for six months.

Mr. West: Yes, there's a single bed, a wardrobe, a desk, a chair and a bookcase.

Gao Bin: And what about the kitchen? You see, I'm Chinese so I'd like to cook for myself because I'm not used to Western food.

Mr. West: Ah, you're from China, are you? I've heard Chinese food is delicious. The kitchen has most things but it doesn't have one of those special Chinese pans. What are they called again?

Gao Bin: You mean a wok?

Mr. West: Yes, that's right, wok. But there's a Chinese supermarket near here so you should be able to buy one from there.

Gao Bin: Is there really a Chinese shop nearby? That's useful.

Mr. West: Oh, yes. This is quite a cosmopolitan area. I think you'll like it.

Gao Bin: I hope so. I have another couple of questions though. Is there a television in the house?

Mr. West: Yes, yes there is. It's in the living room downstairs.

Gao Bin: And what about a telephone?

Mr. West: Yes, but it's a payphone, I'm afraid. You have to pay for your calls as you make them.

Gao Bin: I see. That sounds reasonable. Are water, gas and electricity included in the rent?

Mr. West: Yes, they are. But the rent is negotiable. We can discuss it after you've seen the place.

Gao Bin: That's very kind of you. I still have one more question. I work at the B. G. E building in the centre of town. Is there a direct bus from the house?

Mr. West: Well, you could walk there in half an hour. But there is a bus... Bus 57.

Gao Bin: Right. It sounds ideal. Could I come and see the house this afternoon?

Mr. West: Yes, of course. Would two o'clock suit you?... (*fade out*)

Gao Bin: OK. See you... (*fade out*)

 **Part 3: Track 002** （請配合030、031頁及音檔使用）

Mrs. Kingsley: Are you looking at the house? Nice, isn't it?

Gao Bin: Yes, it is very pleasant.

Mrs. Kingsley: I live here, next door. Have you come to look at Mr. West's rooms?

Gao Bin: Yes, that's right. Do you know Mr. West?

Mrs. Kingsley: Yes, of course I do. I've lived in this area for 45 years. I moved here when I got married. Mr. West and his wife used to live in the house themselves, you know, but they moved to a smaller place a couple of years ago. Mr. West used to help me with odd jobs from time to time, but I don't see him so often now. I still see his son, of course.

Gao Bin: Does his son still live here?

Mrs. Kingsley: As far as I know, yes. I often see him and a couple of his friends leaving the house when they are going to play football.

Gao Bin: Ah, yes. I noticed some people playing football when I walked past the park.

Mrs. Kingsley: OK, the park is lovely, isn't it? We old folks often go there for a walk and a chat, and to watch the children having fun. I'm Jean Kingsley, by the way.

Gao Bin: Pleased to meet you, Mrs. Kingsley. I hope we'll be neighbours. My name's Gao Bin.

Mrs. Kingsley: You can just call me Jean. And where are you from?

Gao Bin: I'm from China.

Mrs. Kingsley: I thought you might be. This will be a good area for you to live in. There's a Chinese supermarket just down the road there...

Gao Bin: Yes, and it seems a nice friendly area.

Mrs. Kingsley: Yes, it is. I wouldn't live anywhere else. There's a library just round the corner where you can read newspapers and magazines. And the community centre is to the right of the library. You can also find some newspapers and magazines there.

Gao Bin: I like the idea of having a newspaper delivered.

Mrs. Kingsley: Well, that's easy enough. There's a newsagent's just down the street.

Gao Bin: And is there a laundry nearby?

Mrs. Kingsley: A laundry? You should do your own washing! You're not made of money, are you? There's a launderette where you can wash your own clothes just beside the library.

Gao Bin:	That's good to know... You're giving me lots of useful information. Let's hope Mr. West will let me have a room.
Mrs. Kingsley:	That shouldn't be a problem. You seem an honest enough chap to me!
Gao bin:	Thank you, and thank you for all your help! I'd better knock on the door now. It's already two o'clock and I don't want to keep Mr. West waiting.
Mrs. Kingsley:	Right, dear. Off you go. I'm here if you need me. I enjoyed talking to you.
Gao Bin:	Bye and thanks again.
Mrs. Kingsley:	Bye.

 第一單元總復習: Track 003 （請配合069頁及音檔使用）

The New Neighbour

Neil:	Oh, hello. I wonder if I could bother you a minute. I've just moved into the flat next door.
Neighbour:	Oh, yes. That's Alice Reilly's old flat. We wondered when we'd be getting a new neighbour. So, you're renting the flat, are you?
Neil:	Yes, that's right. And... er... I was just wondering if I could ask you some questions about the amenities here. Er... like the rubbish collection, for instance.
Neighbour:	Ah, the rubbish is collected on Mondays and Thursdays. You need to put your bin out on the pavement in front of the building the night before, as they come very early... around seven o'clock.

Neil: I see, and what about the stair cleaning. When do the cleaners come? And how do I pay for them?

Neighbour: Oh, they come every Friday morning. Now, if you're going to be out at work, you can leave the money here with me, that's what Mr. Brown from No. 4 does. I'm retired now, so I'm always here when they call, so I'll give it to them for you.

Neil: Oh, thanks very much. How much is it?

Neighbour: It's £1.50 per flat every week.

Neil: OK, and you pay them weekly?

Neighbour: Yes, that's right.

Neil: Well, I have a few more questions. Um... about the neighbourhood mainly. Is there a dry cleaner's near here? I'm desperate to get my shirts cleaned.

Neighbour: Oh, dry cleaner's... let me see now... I don't use them much myself. Ah yes, there's one just down the street on the left... about two blocks down. They're open till about 8 in the evening. I remember now. I had my winter coat cleaned there.

Neil: Oh, that's great. What about the post office? Is there one near here?

Neighbour: Yes, that's very near. Turn right out of the building and it's... er... about 100 yards down, across the road.

Neil: Great. There's just one other thing. If I do get round to doing my washing, is there somewhere I can hang it out to dry?

Neighbour: Didn't the agent tell you? We have a lovely drying green out the back.

Neil: No. I saw the back garden, but he didn't tell me it was communal.

Neighbour: Well, you should have a key to the back door downstairs and that leads out into the garden.

Neil: Oh, I'll have a look at the keys he gave me.

Neighbour: Oh, yes, it's lovely out there. In fact I quite often sit out there and read my newspaper when the weather's good. Oh, that's another thing... we share the cost of the gardener who keeps the grass cut and does the flower beds. That's £5 a month for each flat. He only comes once a month.

Neil: Oh, should I give that money to you too?

Neighbour: Well, he usually comes the first Saturday of each month, so if you know you won't be here, you can give it to me.

Neil: Well, thank you very much. You've been most kind.

Neighbour: Oh, not at all. I'm sure we'll be seeing more of each other.

NOTE

Unit 2 生活與人際關係 Life and Relationships

Unit 2 生活與人際關係

Life and Relationships

　　你是住在學校宿舍還是公寓呢？或者擁有自己的獨棟別墅？這些都是組成一個城市或鄉村的一部分。現在社會越來越進步，我們所居住的社區裡面，服務機構和設備也都更加完善。世界上還有哪些種類的房屋？讓我們一起來看看在社區裡會遇到的各種狀況用英語怎麼說，使你的英語口語表達更加流利。

十年英語不白學，
「各式各樣的人際關係」你怎麼說？

　　在社會中，人與人之間有各式各樣的關係。你能想出哪些類別的人際關係呢？請在下方空白處列出。我已經幫你寫出一個例子了！

 描述各種不同的人際關係。

1. *parents and children*　　　2.

3.　　　　　　　　　　　　　　4.

5.　　　　　　　　　　　　　　6.

7.　　　　　　　　　　　　　　8.

提示與解析

你列出了幾項呢？你可能會提到世代之間的關係，如：parents and children，grandparents and grandchildren，也可能會提到上下級之間的關係，如：employers and employees，還可能會提到兩性之間的關係，如：husband and wife，boyfriend and girlfriend 等。其實，只要有人的地方，就會有人際關係。

Part 1——
社交英語無師自通，道地的「討論私人問題」該怎麼說？

十年英語不白學，「想詢問對方較私人的問題時」就這麼說

　　在非正式場合結交新朋友時，總需要了解對方的一些個人資訊。我們會想知道對方有沒有男友或女友，有沒有結婚，有沒有孩子等。當然這些問題都是私人問題，詢問他人時要注意禮貌。以下列出了一些常見問題。仔細閱讀這些問題，再看一看下一頁方框中的答句，將問題與答案互相搭配起來。有些問題的答案可能不只一個。請將恰當答句的字母寫在問題旁邊的橫線上。我已經為你做好第一題了！

將問題與答案搭配起來。

Question	Answer(s)
❶ Are you going out with anybody?	A, J
❷ Do you have a boyfriend?	_____
❸ Are you married?	_____
❹ How long have you been engaged?	_____
❺ Do you have (any) children?	_____
❻ Where did you meet you wife?	_____
❼ How long have you been married?	_____
❽ When are you getting married?	_____

A. No, not at the moment.　　　B. Probably towards the end of next year.

C. Not anymore. I was divorced 18 months ago.

D. Not yet! We're getting married in June.　　E. Yeah! I got married last year.

F. No, not yet. We're hoping to start a family next year.

G. You must be joking! I'm having too much fun being single!

H. About six months.　　　I. At work. We used to be colleagues.

J. Yes, I am. In fact, I'm engaged.　　　K. Next year, I hope.

L. Three years... and we already have a daughter.

$\boxed{\text{提示與解析}}$

答得如何呢？相信你一定覺得有些題目比較難，而有些比較簡單吧。

• 第**2**題：前兩題非常類似，但第**1**題的答案可以是J或A，第**2**題的答案只能
　　　是A（為什麼J不行？因為問句與答句動詞要一致，仔細看一看吧）。

• 第**3**題：A、C、D、E、G都是可能的答案。

• 第**4**題：因為題目裡有 "how long"，所以答案必須是「一段時間」，因此答案是
　　　H，L雖然也包含「一段時間」，但是不太符合常情，所以這個答案不
　　　太合適。

• 第**5**題：F

• 第**6**題：I

• 第**7**題：H或L都可以。

• 第**8**題：K或B都可以。

　　前面說了，以上這些問題都是私人問題，在問這些問題時總要小心點，最好不要在一大群人面前問，否則對方會不好意思。我們在問私人問題時，常會搭配一些句型來避免冒犯他人。請看下方的例子。

I hope you don't mind me asking but are you married?
（希望你不介意我問，你結婚了嗎？）

Forgive me for asking but do you have a boyfriend?
（請原諒我這麼問，你有男朋友嗎？）

Excuse my curiosity but do you have children?
（請原諒我這麼好奇，你有孩子嗎？）

　　畫了底線的部分，可以在問任何私人問題時使用。問題的語序不會因為加了這部分而改變。

拒當英文句點王，換你練習開口說說看！

我們錄製了一些其他詢問他人個人資訊的問題，仔細聽音檔，試著練習詢問個人資訊，注意發音與音調。 ◀ *Track 004*

Part 2—
社交英語無師自通，
道地的「婚姻故事」該怎麼說？

你知道什麼是 "dialogue" 嗎？你知道什麼是 "monologue" 嗎？它們分別是對話和獨白。在下面的練習中，我們會讀到兩段 "monologue"。這種獨白近年來常出現在雜誌中，通常都是雜誌編輯在採訪名人後寫下的。獨白多以第一人稱來寫，會讓人感覺比較親切，也比較私密。在讀這類獨白時，你會看到不同人之間的人際關係。你會發現，這些獨白中涵蓋了很多內容，也用了不少口語的說法。

以下提供了一些概略性的主題。快速讀一遍以下的獨白（Text 1 和 Text 2），判斷這兩段獨白分別屬於哪個主題。在最適當的選項前打勾。

 在兩段獨白的主題旁打個勾。

( ) ⓐ Parents and children
( ) ⓑ Friends
( ) ⓒ Marriage partners and lovers
( ) ⓓ Employers and employees

 —Text 1

Cliff is 29 years old. He was born in California.

I was married for almost six years—happily married for the first two years. Jody and I were classmates at high school and were attracted to each other from the time we first met at the age of twelve or thirteen. We always hung out together and started dating seriously when we were only fifteen. I was so excited the first time I asked her out! After that, we spent every spare moment together.

Everyone—our parents, teachers, friends and so on—predicted that we'd break up one day. We were determined to prove them wrong and were engaged when we were nineteen. The evening I proposed was like something from a romantic novel. I chose my moment and asked the magic question, "Jody, darling, will you marry me?" Her answer was a few tears of happiness. It seems crazy when I look back on it! Again, everyone was expecting us to break off the engagement but we never even considered that.

A year later, we had a typical, big wedding ceremony and Jody really did look the perfect, beautiful bride in her white gown. We had a great time in Lake Tahoe for our honeymoon and came back and settled down to married life. Jessica, our daughter, was born, according to plan, two years after we were married and that was when our problems began.

We were both delighted to be parents but somehow we just grew further and further apart from each other. We were arguing the whole time and were both very miserable. Eventually, after four years, we separated and then, divorced. I still see Jessica regularly. I can't say I enjoy living alone but I haven't yet found another partner. Jody is dating a guy who lives in the same apartment house as her but I don't think their relationship is really serious. I'm really sad about our divorce but I guess everyone was right: we were too young when we started going together and, the truth is, we were never really compatible.

Text 2

34-year-old Winston was born in London.

After ten years of marriage, I still feel really happy about my life with Lucy. I think she's the best woman in the world. I can't say I've never looked at another woman since I met her but I've truly never wanted anyone else!

I was really wild when I was younger. I went out to clubs and discos all the time, and drank lots of beer and had fun. I never had much luck with girls. I went out with lots of different girls but they always tired of my wild ways and ended the relationships after a month or two. I usually chose black women. I find them attractive and always thought white women wouldn't be interested in me because I'm black—from a West Indian background—and, whatever people say, there has been lots of prejudice against us.

I'll never forget the first time I saw Lucy—at a disco in Camden. I couldn't take my eyes off her. I'd never really fancied a white woman before but I thought she was absolutely fantastic. I guess it was probably "love at first sight". We've been together ever since! There were a few problems with her parents at first. I wasn't the sort of guy they'd imagined having as a son-in-law but they soon got used to me and realised how happy Lucy and I were together.

I asked her to marry me after we'd been going out together for about four months. I could only afford a cheap engagement ring but she didn't mind at all. Six months later, we were married. The wedding was a very simple one in a registry office but we had a great party afterwards. We couldn't afford a honeymoon but that didn't bother us.

Now, three children later, we're still having fun together. I'm not saying we've never had any problems. The occasional disagreement is only natural. Our worst rows are on Sunday mornings. I usually try to have a long sleep and Lucy gets a bit angry with me because she has to deal with the children, single-handed. But we usually make it up by lunchtime and, it's great, Lucy never sulks. She speaks her mind and then forgets the problem. As I say, she's fantastic and I can't imagine life without her.

提示與解析

你應該很快就發現了，這兩段文字都和 "Marriage partners and lovers（婚姻伴侶與情人）" 相關。雖然英文中會使用 "relationship" 這個字來指兩個人之間的關係，但 "relationship" 同時也可以用來專指兩人之間的愛情。我們常用 "They're having a relationship." 來表示兩個人有超出友誼的關係。在這個單元中，我們主要探討這種關係。

十年英語不白學，「敘述故事」就這麼說

現在請閱讀Text 1和Text 2這兩篇獨白，並從以下五個標題中，選擇適合搭配這兩篇獨白的標題。把相應的篇名寫在對應標題的右側橫線上，並在其他沒有用到的標題旁的橫線上打叉。

 為 **Text 1** 和 **Text 2** 選出恰當的標題。

Titles	Text Number
A Happy Marriage	_____
The Happy Bachelor	_____
A Failed Marriage	_____
Unlucky in Love	_____
Twice Divorced	_____

提示與解析

在 Text 1中，我們發現克利夫（Cliff）的婚姻並不幸福。從第一段的第一句、最後一段的第一句和最後兩句中都可以看出這一點。在 Text 2 中，我們發現溫斯頓（Winston）的婚姻很幸福，從第一段的第一句、最後一段的第一句和最後一句中都可以看出這一點。因此，答案是：A Failed Marriage: Text 1; A Happy Marriage: Text 2。

透過這個練習，想必你一定會發現讀文章時第一句話和最後一句話很重要。

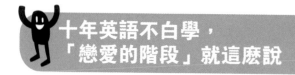

一段戀愛，主要會有以下這些階段：
- They met.　他們相遇了。
- They went out together. (They split up.) 他們開始約會。（他們分手了。）
- They got engaged. (They split up.) 他們訂婚了。（他們分手了。）
- They got married. (They split up.) 他們結婚了。（他們分手了。）
- They "lived happily ever after". / They are still together. (They divorced.)
  他們幸福地生活在一起。/ 他們還在一起。（他們離婚了。）

也就是說，在以上任何一個階段，一對情侶或夫妻都有可能分手，或繼續朝著下一個階段邁進。

閱讀 Text 1 和 Text 2，利用以上句子概述其中發生的主要事件。

概述 Text 1 和 Text 2:

Text 1

_____

_____

_____

_____

_____

Text 2

_____

_____

_____

_____

_____

提示與解析

Text 1
Cliff and Jody met.
They went out together.

They got engaged.
They got married.
They divorced.
Text 2
Winston and Lucy met.
They went out together.
They got engaged.
They got married.
They are still together.

你會發現前面我們寫到 "lived happily ever after" 的時候，加了引號，為什麼呢？這是因為在西方的童話故事中，故事常常以 "lived happily ever after" 結束。因此，在這裡加上引號，是一種幽默的方式描述婚姻生活。

　　閱讀下面的句子，將敘述句與其所描述的人物正確配對。其中有些句子描述的是克利夫（Cliff）和喬蒂（Jody）的生活，有些描述的則是溫斯頓（Winston）與露西（Lucy）的生活，還有些都不是。請在描述克利夫與喬蒂的句子旁寫下「CJ」，在描述溫斯頓與露西的句子旁寫下「WL」。還有些句子兩者都符合，請在旁邊寫下「CJ / WL」。如果兩者皆不符合，則在旁邊畫叉。

 將下面句子與其所描述的人物配對。

❶ They met at work. _____

❷ They met at school. _____

❸ They met in a disco. _____

❹ The boy was immediately attracted to the girl. _____

❺ Their parents weren't very happy about the relationship. _____

❻ They had a big wedding. _____

⑦ They had a small church wedding. _____

⑧ They didn't go away for a honeymoon. _____

⑨ They've been married for six years. _____

⑩ They've been married for ten years. _____

⑪ They were married for six years. _____

⑫ They have three children. _____

提示與解析

克利夫與喬迪（CJ）：❷,❹,❺,❻,⑪

溫斯頓與露西（WL）：❸,❹,❺,❽,⑩,⑫

兩者都不：❶,❼,❾

十年英語不白學，「描述事件發生的時間」就這麼說

　　兩篇文章都依照時間的先後順序（chronological）描述了發生的事情。大部分的動詞都用了一般過去式。兩篇的最後一段也都與「現在」有關。

　　在提到過去的事情時，描述時間的片語和時間副詞就非常重要，因為它們能幫助聽者了解事件發生的先後順序。

　　看看以下這個例子（引自 Text 2）：

Six months later, we were married.

要完全了解這個句子，我們必須回頭看看 Text 2，才知道六個月前到底發生了什麼事。原來，六個月前溫斯頓和露西訂婚了（文章中沒有直接說出來，但提到了溫斯頓要露西嫁給他，還拿出了訂婚戒指，所以我們可以猜測他們是訂婚了）。

接下來就請你看看 Text 1，並根據時間片語與時間副詞，寫出以下事件發生的時間。

根據 Text 1 填入適當的時間片語。

❶ We started dating seriously *when we were only fifteen*.

❷ _____, we spent every spare moment together.

❸ We were engaged _____.

❹ _____, we had a typical, big wedding ceremony.

❺ Jessica was born _____.

❻ _____, we separated _____, divorced.

提示與解析

❷ After that
❸ when we were nineteen
❹ A year later
❺ two years after we were married
❻ After four years;and then

　　請注意："after" 後面可以接名詞或名詞片語（如：four years，ten years of marriage），還可以接一個子句（如：we were married），或只接 "that" 一個字。如果要搞清楚 "that" 到底是指什麼，就要仔細看看上文。

　　"later" 可以單獨使用（什麼都不接），但一般而言，在描述事件時，通常前面會接上一段「時間」（如：10 minutes later，two years later，three weeks later等）。你可能會注意到，Text 2 中用了 "three children later"。用這種說法來描述時間並不常見，但相信你應該可以猜出來，它就是「有了三個孩子之後」的意思。

　　"then" 是用來描述事情先後順序的，通常用來連接兩件發生時間間隔較短的事。

　　請注意和這些描述時間的說法一起出現的標點符號。當這些描述時間的說法出現在句子最前面時，後面會跟一個逗號，如果出現在句子最後面，就不需要逗號了。舉例來說：

Three years later, **they were married.**

They were married three years later.

十年英語不白學，「不同階段的感情狀態」就這麼說

　　你可能會注意到，在這兩篇文章中，作者用了不同的說法來描述感情狀態的不同階段。

　　以下方框裡的說法，都是在這兩篇文章中出現過的。在文章中把它們找出來畫上底線，並猜猜看它們的意思。這些說法依據感情的不同階段，可以歸為四類。方框中的說法究竟各屬於哪一類？請寫下來。

A. to grow apart

B. to tire of

C. to go out with

D. to go together

E. to date

F. to fancy

G. to find somebody attractive

H. to start dating

I. to be attracted to each other

J. to separate

K. to hang out together

L. to divorce

M. to be together

N. to take somebody out

O. to be unable to take one's eyes off

P. to ask somebody out

Q. to fall in love at first sight

R. to be interested in

S. to go out together

 將以上的說法歸類到以下四類中。

Stage 1:   <u>Before the relationship actually begins</u> (6 expressions)

_____

Stage 2:   <u>Making the first move / Beginning the relationship</u> (2 expressions)

_____

Stage 3:   <u>Spending time together / Having a relationship</u> (7 expressions)

_____

Stage 4:   <u>Ending the relationship</u> (4 expressions)

_____

提示與解析

Stage 1:> 在一段感情開始前（before a relationship begins），可以用以下這些說法描述兩人之間相互吸引、感興趣：F, G, I, O, Q, R。

Stage 2:> 感情剛踏出第一步可以說：H, P。

Stage 3:> 兩人在交往中可以說：C, D, E, K, M, N, S。

Stage 4:> 結束一段感情可以說：A, B, J, L。

此外，要描述一段感情結束，也可以用 "to split up" 或 "to break up" 來表達。
無論是正在交往階段，或者已經訂婚或結婚，都有可能 "split up" 或 "break
up"。

社交英語無師自通，你一定還想知道更多！

　　順帶一提，「求婚」的英文你知道怎麼說嗎？是 "p" 開頭的，想想看！另
外，courting / courtship 這些說法，是用來描述兩人「在交往」，但還沒有
結婚。這些說法比較老式了，通常只有年紀大的人會用（他們可能會說：
Are you courting?）你不需要真的在日常生活中用這些說法（甚至建議你最
好不要用）。想一想可以換用什麼其他的說法呢？

 十年英語不白學，
「故事摘要」就這麼說

　　再次閱讀 Text 1，先從文章中找出需要的資訊，用筆記的形式完成下面的表
格。第一部分已經幫你填好了。這項表格的資訊在後面練習寫摘要時會用上。

 閱讀 Text 1，完成表格。

Cliff's Marriage

❶ when & where they met	when 12 or 13, at school
❷ when first attracted to each other	

❸ when engaged	
❹ when married	
❺ when their daughter was born	
❻ what happened after the birth	
❼ result	
❽ length of marriage	
❾ Cliff's attitude to the result	

提示與解析

表格中的筆記只要你自己看得懂就好，所以不一定要用什麼完整的表達，只要確定把重點都寫下來。我可能會這樣寫：

❷ the first time they met
❸ (when they were) 19
❹ a year later
❺ after two years / two years after marriage
❻ problems began / argued / grew apart
❼ separated / divorced
❽ six years
❾ sad

現在我們來想想，如果要寫這兩篇文章的摘要（summary），應該怎麼寫呢？先讀讀下面的摘要，這個摘要是用前一個練習表格中填好的資訊完成的 。讀一讀，看看這篇摘要是怎麼組織的，你會發現大部分句子都很精簡！

 想想看寫摘要的過程。

Cliff and Jody met at school when they were only 12 or 13 years old. They were attracted to each other from the first time they met. They got engaged at 19. They got married one year later. Two years later, their first daughter was born. After her birth, they often argued and grew further and further apart. Finally, they separated and then divorced. They were married for almost six years. Cliff feels sad about his unsuccessful marriage.

你會發現，在寫摘要時，只要挑出重點就好，不用寫得太詳細。寫摘要前可以先做好筆記，這樣會比較清楚該寫哪些東西。之前關於克利夫的表格就等於是做了很好的筆記。當然，你不一定要畫一個很漂亮的表格，但還是得先想好你在摘要中到底要寫下哪些資訊。

十年英語不白學，
「婚姻生活的摘要」就這麼說

在後面的練習中，我們將要請你完成一份關於溫斯頓的婚姻的摘要，所以在這個練習中就要先做好準備！閱讀85頁的 Text 2，完成以下表格。

閱讀**Text 2**，完成以下表格。

Winston's Marriage

❶ length of marriage	
❷ where first met Lucy	
❸ when engaged	
❹ when & where married	
❺ number of children	
❻ his feelings for his wife	
❼ his attitude towards their marriage	

現在你已經做好準備，可以開始為溫斯頓的婚姻生活寫一份摘要了。在寫這份摘要時，請你仔細想想動詞時態該怎麼用。要記得，前面提到的克利夫離婚了，但溫斯頓跟他太太現在還是恩恩愛愛的，所以有時候會描述到「現在」發生的事情，有時也會描述「過去」的事情。因此，你就必須思考，到底該用 "They have been married for..."，還是 "They were married for..."。記得要適時使用描述時間的說法來表達每個事件之間的關聯。把你的摘要寫在下頁的空白之處，請參考你之前完成的關於克利夫婚姻生活的表格，以及關於克利夫婚姻生活的摘要。

為溫斯頓的婚姻生活寫一篇摘要。

Winston's Marriage

你在寫第一句的時候，時態寫對了嗎？你在描述兩人見面、訂婚、結婚時，正確地使用過去式了嗎？在描述他們現在有幾個孩子、溫斯頓現在對他太太的感情、對他婚姻生活的想法時，正確地使用現在式了嗎？要小心確認！如果用錯了，可以回頭看看之前提到的時態規則。然後再為自己打個分數，滿分十分的話，你會給自己多少分呢？

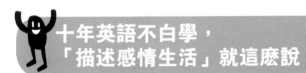

十年英語不白學，「描述感情生活」就這麼說

　　結束這項活動之前，你可以花一點時間自己練習說說英文。想想自己的感情生活（如果你有男女朋友或另一半的話），以及你身旁其他人的感情生活。試試看為這些感情生活也做個摘要，要記得使用在這項練習中學到的表達方式。

拒當英文句點王，換你練習開口說說看！

開口練習談論各種不同的感情生活。

　　試著為這些感情生活寫一篇摘要。

Part 3——
社交英語無師自通，
道地的「採訪和面談」該怎麼說？

在前一個練習中，我們以雜誌文章為基礎，討論了各種不同的感情生活。當時提到，雜誌的文章雖然是用「第一人稱」寫的，彷彿是從受訪者本人口中說出，但其實文章還是由雜誌的編輯或記者寫的。編輯或記者為了寫出文章，一定問了克利夫和溫斯頓很多問題。在下面的練習中，我們會學到一些問問題的方法。

為了寫好雜誌文章，採訪者必須要問一些很精確的問題，才能得到最精確的答案，寫出完整的文章。因此，在採訪前，採訪人做了筆記提醒自己該問什麼。看看這份筆記，想像一下，採訪人究竟問了哪些問題？每個問題可以用很多不同的方式提問，請你想出一些最可能、最常見的問法，寫在每項筆記下面的空白處。第一題已經為你寫好了。

 寫下這位採訪者可能問了哪些問題。

❶ when they met

When did you meet?
_____

❷ where they met

_____

❸ when first attracted to each other

_____

④ where married

_____

⑤ length of marriage

_____

⑥ when engaged

_____

⑦ honeymoon

_____

⑧ his feelings for his wife

_____

⑨ his feelings about the marriage / divorce

_____

⑩ what happened after the marriage / birth / divorce

_____

提示與解析

相信這些問題中大部分不難吧！

② Where did you meet?
③ When were you first attracted to each other?
④ Where were you married? 或 Where did you get married?
⑤ How long have you been married?（用於目前仍在結婚狀態的人）
　或 How long were you married?（用於已離婚的人）
⑥ When did you get engaged? 或 When were you engaged?（較少見的問法）

7 Did you have a honeymoon? 或 Did you go away for a honeymoon?

8 How do you feel about your wife?

9 How do you feel about your marriage / divorce?

　或 What are your feelings about your marriage / divorce?

10 What happened after the marriage / birth / divorce?

社交英語無師自通，你一定還想知道更多！

　　你會發現，有不少問題中出現了 "did"。可以看出，這些題目都是問「過去的事」。你可能也注意到了，問到「婚姻」的時候，出現了兩種問法：...were you married? /...did you get married? 這是因為結婚可以說 "be married"，也可以說 "get married"。在婚禮的時候，可以說一對新人 "is married by the vicar（教區牧師）/ priest（神父）/ registrar（登記人員）", 也可以說他們 "get married to each other"。前者是「被動語氣（passive voice）」，後者是「主動語氣（active voice）」。

　　請注意，"How do you feel about...?" 是個很有用的問句句型，無論討論的是什麼話題幾乎都可以用。還可以拿來問過去的事，只是要把 "do" 改成過去式did，即：How did you feel about...? 此外，"What happened?" 也是個很好用的問法。你可以做很多變化：What happened next?（接下來發生了什麼事？）What happened then?（當時發生了什麼事？）What happened after that?（那之後發生了什麼事？）

　　採訪了克利夫和溫斯頓的雜誌記者後來也採訪了蘇珊（Susan），她是個來自曼徹斯特的28歲教師。以下列出的是這位採訪者在訪問蘇珊時記下的筆記。從筆記中，你可不可以推測出記者究竟問了哪些問題呢？請根據答案找出相對應的問題。你可以復習一下之前的活動中練習過的問題。第一題已經為你寫好了。

1 Q: <u>Are you married?</u>

A: No, divorced.

2 Q: _____

A: Only two years.

3 Q: _____

A: Terrible. The break-up was very upsetting.

4 Q: _____

A: Yes... but it's not very serious.

5 Q: _____

A: About six months ago.

6 Q: _____

A: In a pub, through friends.

7 Q: _____

A: After a few weeks... I didn't fancy him at first.

8 Q: _____

A: Fine, he's a nice, kind guy... but not very handsome.

❷ 既然前一題說到蘇珊已經離婚，這一題的筆記又提到了「只有兩年」，我們可以判斷訪問者很可能問了：How long were you married?（你們的婚姻持續了多久？）

❸ How do / did you feel about the divorce?（你對離婚的感受如何？這個問題有可能用了過去式，也可能用了現在式。）

❹ 這題有很多可能的答案：

Do you have a boyfriend / partner at the moment?（你現在有男友 / 情人嗎？）

或 Are you going out with anyone at the moment?（你現在有在交往的對象嗎？）

❺ When did you meet him (the guy / the man / your new partner, etc.)?（你們什麼時候認識的？）

❻ Where did you meet him?（你在哪裡遇見他的？）

❼ When were you first attracted to each other?（你們從什麼時候開始互相吸引？）

❽ How do you feel about him?（你對他感覺如何？）

最後提醒一下：關於私人問題，一般情況下，一定要確定不會冒犯到對方時才能提問。

Part 4——
社交英語無師自通，
道地的「討論婚禮計劃」該怎麼說？

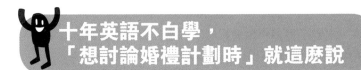

十年英語不白學，
「想討論婚禮計劃時」就這麼說

聽聽看露絲（Ruth）與莎倫（Sharon）的對話。聽第一遍的時候，試著習慣她們的聲音，並根據下面列出的問題抓住這段對話的大意。記得在聽音檔前要先把問題都讀一遍。

🔊 聽音檔，回答問題。　◀≷*Track 005*

❶ Can you guess what they talked about previously?

❷ Which of the following is the main topic of the conversation? Choose one only.
   A. A wedding ceremony in a registry office
   B. Honeymoons
   C. Ruth's marriage
   D. The personality of Ruth's ex-husband
   E. Sharon's wedding dress

提示與解析

第❶題應該不難答，因為在對話剛開始時，莎倫說：" ...thanks for showing such interest in all my plans..."（謝謝你對我的計劃這麼感興趣）。從這裡可以輕鬆判斷，兩人之前討論了莎倫的婚禮計劃。

第❷題的正確答案是 C，因為整段對話大部分的內容都是在講露絲的婚姻生活。雖然兩人也有提到結婚登記、露絲的前夫、婚禮要穿的禮服等，但這些小細節都不是這段對話的重點。

露絲在這段對話中，提到了很多和她婚姻有關的事。閱讀下面每一對句子，在符合露絲情形的句子後打勾。如果需要，可以再聽一遍音檔。

🔊 勾出正確的句子。 ◀ *Track 005*

❶ Ruth is married.( )
 Ruth is divorced.( )

❷ She was married in a church.( )
 She was married in a registry office.( )

❸ It was a big wedding.( )
 It was a small wedding.( )

❹ She wore a loose, cream dress.( )
 She wore a tight, cream dress.( )

❺ She was 17 years old.( )
 She was 27 years old.( )

❻ Frankie was handsome.( )
 Frankie was unattractive.( )

❼ He was a good husband.(　　)
He was a terrible husband.(　　)

❽ Ruth's parents made her feel guilty.(　　)
Ruth's parents were good to her.(　　)

提示與解析

1 Ruth is divorced.
2 She was married in a registry office.
3 It was a small wedding.
4 She wore a loose, cream dress.
5 She was 17 years old.
6 Frankie was handsome.
7 He was a terrible husband.
8 Ruth's parents were good to her.

從這些答案中，你應該也可以大概判斷出整段對話的重點了吧！
你聽出為什麼露絲結婚時穿著一件寬鬆的婚紗嗎？因為她在結婚時就已經懷孕了。莎倫在提到這件事的時候說：「你是不是不得不結婚啊？」也就是在隱晦地表示：你是不是懷孕了所以不得不結婚啊？這個說法現在算是比較老式了，但還是有些人會使用。另一種說法是 "shotgun wedding"，描述的是「因為懷孕了所以趕快結婚」的那種婚禮。

十年英語不白學，
「想描述他人的婚禮時」就這麼說

你現在對露絲的婚姻很了解了吧！做好筆記後，把露絲感情生活的種種階段寫下來。你可以參考之前在討論克利夫以及溫斯頓婚姻時填的表格。現在請以露絲的身份寫一段（七到八句）第一人稱的獨白，描述她的感情與婚姻生活。請用 "I met Frankie..." 作為開頭。

 寫一段描述露絲（Ruth）與弗蘭克（Frankie）感情與婚姻的文章。

請使用如下標題：

<u>**My Marriage**</u>

_____

_____

_____

_____

_____

_____

_____

_____

_____

_____

_____

提示與解析

I met Frankie when I was 15 years old. He completely swept me off my feet the first time we met at a party. He was also attracted by me and called me 「Miss Cheerful」. We soon hung out together. I was pregnant when I was 17 and had a shotgun marriage with Frankie that year. We married in a registry office. It turned out that he made a terrible husband and father. Our daughter was born five months after the wedding and Frankie left me a month later.

十年英語不白學， 「想表達主觀和客觀想法」就這麼說

　　你在音檔中聽到的對話其實還是比較私人的。其中你可以聽出許多不同的情緒。下面列出了一些句子，這些句子都在對話中出現過。再聽一遍對話，判斷這些句子是用來問一些比較敏感的問題，還是用來表達惋惜、後悔之意，還是用來表達同情或者只是冷靜客觀地給出評論。也就是說，請你判斷這些句子的「功能（function）」。在每個句子旁邊寫下正確的答案（A、B、C或D）。第一題已經為你做好了！

> Functions
> A. asking "delicate" questions
> B. expressing regrets
> C. showing sympathy
> D. making comments

聽音檔，寫下這些說法在對話中的功能。 ◀ *Track 005*

[B] ❶ I would have loved a big wedding.

[ ] ❷ You don't mind me asking, do you?

[ ] ❸ Forgive me for asking, but weren't your parents there?

[ ] ❹ I wish I hadn't been so silly.

[ ] ❺ Don't be so hard on yourself!

[ ] ❻ Excuse my curiosity but what's his name?

[ ] ❼ I just wish I'd never met him.

[ ] ❽ I wish I'd told him to "get lost" then.

[ ] ❾ You poor thing...

[ ] ❿ You must have been terrified.

[ ] ⓫ I'm so sorry.

[ ] ⓬ There are a million things I wish I'd done.

[ ] ⓭ I've never thought of you as a sad person.

[ ] ⓮ Things could have been worse.

提示與解析

A（問敏感的問題）：❷ 、❸ 、❻
B（表達惋惜、後悔）：❶ 、❹ 、❼ 、❽ 、⓬
C（表達同情）：❺ 、❾ 、⓫
D（表達評論）：❿ 、⓭ 、⓮

要注意的是，❺ 和❿ 既包含了同情與精神上支持，也有評論的意思，所以把 ❺ 和 ❿ 列在C類或D類都沒問題。

十年英語不白學， 「想表達後悔時」就這麼說

可憐的露絲似乎對很多事情都很後悔，看看前一個練習中的這些句子就知道：

I would have loved a big wedding. （我真希望當時能辦一場盛大的婚禮。）
I wish I hadn't been so silly. （我真希望自己當時沒那麼蠢。）
I just wish I'd never met him. （我真希望自己根本沒認識過他。）
I wish I'd told him to "get lost" then. （我真希望我當時就叫他滾了。）
There are a million things I wish I'd done. （我真希望當時去做了很多很多事。）

聽音檔，寫下六件露絲希望自己當時能做的事。請看如下提示：a big wedding，a white dress，a good husband，university，travel，good job。請用以下的句型：She wishes she'd had an expensive reception.

🔊 聽音檔，寫下句子，描述露絲希望自己曾經能夠去做的事。
◀ *Track 005*

❶ _____

❷ _____

❸ _____

❹ _____

❺ _____

❻ _____

露絲後悔的事有很多，例如：

She wishes she'd never met him.（她真希望自己從來沒遇見過他。）

She wishes she hadn't gone to that party.（她真希望當時沒參加那場聚會。）

以下這些後悔的事並未直接在對話中提到，但我們可以猜到，露絲應該很後悔自己以前中途退學（leave school）、很年輕就懷孕（get pregnant when she was so young）、嫁給弗蘭克。使用以上句型，寫出關於這三件後悔的事情的句子。

 寫下關於這三件後悔的事情的句子。

❼ _____

❽ _____

❾ _____

提示與解析

寫這些句子的時候，最重要的就是要記得在 "wish" 的後面要接過去完成式（past perfect, had + 動詞的過去分詞）。注意每個句子中都要這樣用才行！

❶ She wishes she'd had a big wedding.

❷ She wishes she'd worn a white dress.

❸ She wishes she'd had a good husband.

❹ She wishes she'd gone to university.

　　或 She wishes she'd been to university.

❺ She wishes she had travelled.

❻ She wishes she'd had a good job.

❼ She wishes she hadn't left school (so early).

❽ She wishes she hadn't got pregnant when she was so young.

❾ She wishes she hadn't married Frankie.

十年英語不白學，「用不同的句型表達自己曾後悔的事情」就這麼說

　　我們都有後悔的事，後悔當初沒做某事，後悔當初做了某事。這些事或大或小，或許嚴重，或許輕微。在上一個練習中，你或許發現，可以用不同的句型表達悔意。

　　練習使用以上學到的句型，描述一些讓你覺得後悔的事。可以變換使用 "I wish I'd... / I wish I hadn't... / I would have loved / liked..."（如果當時……有多好 / 我本來想要……）。可以邊寫邊參考露絲在音檔中所說的話。

拒當英文句點王，換你練習開口說說看！
練習說說自己後悔的事。

✎ 如果在腦海裡拼湊有點困難的話，可以拿出筆來列出一些重要的關鍵字幫助自己哦！

_____

_____

_____

_____

_____

_____

Part 5——
社交英語無師自通，
道地的「結婚細節」該怎麼說？

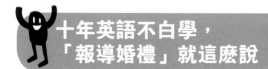

十年英語不白學，
「報導婚禮」就這麼說

下面是從一份英國報紙中摘錄出來的公告。閱讀以下問題，選擇最適當的選項。

 勾出最適當的選項。

❶ What type of newspaper is it from?
   A. An international newspaper.
   B. A national newspaper.
   C. A local newspaper.

❷ Which section of the newspaper do you think it comes from?
   A. The national news section.
   B. The local news section.
   C. The social events diary.
   D. Announcements.
   E. Advertisements.
   F. The crime page.

Harrison / Barlow — Mr. and Mrs. F. Harrison are happy to announce the marriage of their daughter, Jane, to Henry Barlow.

James / Whitley — Alison Whitely and David James were married at Morton registry office. The couple are spending their honeymoon in Thailand.

Wang / Gibson — David Gibson and Wang Yang were married at Morton registry office. Family and friends wish the couple every happiness.

ENGAGEMENTS

Appleby / Watts — Mr. and Mrs. Leslie Appleby offer their congratulations to their daughter, Sharon, on her engagement to Philip Watts.

Nugent / Wilson — Mr. and Mrs. G. Nugent are delighted to announce the engagement of their youngest daughter, Sally, to Colin Wilson, son of Mr. and Mrs. K. Wilson of Chester.

Billings / Hampton — Joe and Liz Hampton are happy to announce the engagement of their daughter, Sophie, to Kenneth Billings.

提示與解析

❶ B 或 C。這篇公告有可能刊登在全國性的（national）報紙上，也可能刊登在地區性的（local）報紙上。一般而言，這樣的公告比較可能刊登在地區性的報紙上，因為這裡面公告的消息並不是每項都有提到「地點」（即：讀者應該都知道婚禮是發生在哪座城市，而全國性報紙的讀者不太可能會知道這種事）。

❷ D。這些公告算是 "announcements"。可能有些同學會選 B，因為這些消息的確也算是「地方新聞」，但一般而言新聞文章通常都會寫出更多的資訊。

閱讀上頁的報紙公告，回答下列問題。

❶ Two types of announcement are included in the extract. You can see one heading: Engagements. What do you think the other heading is?

_____

❷ Two more types of announcement are usually included in this section. What do you think they might be?

_____

提示與解析

❶ 答案是 "Marriages"，也可以說 "Weddings"，不過 "wedding" 這個詞沒有 "marriage" 正式，因為是報紙上的公告，通常會選擇比較正式的說法。

❷ 答案是 "Births" 和 "Deaths"，也就是說，開心的公告和難過的公告可以放在一起。不過，"Divorces" 則不會公告出來。

十年英語不白學，「婚禮細節」就這麼說

　　閱讀下面的兩篇文章，它們是從報紙上摘錄的兩則地方新聞，都詳細描述了最近的婚禮。其中提到的這兩場婚禮，都在前面的報紙公告上出現過。閱讀這兩則新聞，完成表格。 如果表格中要求提供的資訊在文章中並沒有提到，可以直接寫 "not stated"。如果有看不懂的單字，不用擔心，我們在後面的練習中會介紹！第一格已經幫你填好了。

(A)
Marriage at St. Mary's

A hundred and fifty guests attended the marriage ceremony of Jane Francis Harrison, of Morton, and Henry Barlow from Surrey.

Reverend J.H. Casey officiated at St. Mary's church. The bride, who wore a white silk gown and carried a spray of white roses and gypsophila, was given away by her father, Felix Harrison. She was attended by three bridesmaids in pale pink silk dresses, and a page-boy in a sailor suit. The best man was William Barlow, the groom's brother.

After the ceremony, there was a buffet reception at the County Hotel. The happy couple spent the first night of their married life in the hotel, before leaving Morton on Sunday morning, for a honeymoon in Scotland.

(B)
Local man weds Chinese doctor

Guests at Morton registry office on Saturday enjoyed the marriage ceremony of Wang Yang, from Shanghai, China and local man, David Gibson. The couple met three years ago in Manchester, where Wang Yang was studying medicine.

The bride wore a traditional Chinese dress of red silk and carried yellow roses. The witnesses were the bride's close friend, Ling Mei, and the bridegroom's friend, Philip Ward.

An informal reception party for the couple was held at the home of the groom's parents, Mr. And Mrs. Arnold Gibson.

The couple left for a honeymoon in the south of France on Saturday evening.

 請閱讀文章並完成以下表格。

	Wedding A	Wedding B
❶ place of ceremony	church	

	Wedding A	Wedding B
❷ time of ceremony		
❸ No. of guests		
❹ bride's dress		
❺ bride's flowers		
❻ bride was given away by		
❼ No. of bridesmaids		
❽ No. of witnesses		
❾ type of reception		
❿ place of reception		
⓫ place of honeymoon		

提示與解析

Wedding A
① church
❷ Saturday
❸ 150
❹ a white silk gown
❺ white roses
❻ her father
❼ three
❽ not stated
❾ buffet
❿ a hotel
⓫ Scotland

Wedding B
① registry office
❷ Saturday
❸ not stated
❹ a red silk dress
❺ yellow roses
❻ not stated
❼ not stated
❽ two
❾ informal
❿ the home of the groom's parents
⓫ the south of France

十年英語不白學，「關於婚禮的專有名詞」就這麼說

在任何重要場合，都會有扮演不同角色的人，例如婚禮。有些角色還有特殊的專有名稱，而婚禮的某些儀式也有特殊的專有名稱。再次閱讀前面的兩則新聞，找找看，裡面出現了哪些特殊說法。把答案寫在下面的橫線上。第一題已經為你寫好了。

閱讀文章，為以下的人與事填入正確的單字或片語。

❶ The female who is getting married is known as <u>the bride</u>.

❷ The male who is getting married is known as _____.

❸ The female who attends / accompanies the woman who is getting married is known as _____.

❹ The boy who attends the woman who is getting married is known as _____.

❺ The male who attends / accompanies the man who is getting married is known as _____.

❻ The two people who accompany a couple who get married in a registry office are _____.

❼ The other people who attend a wedding are _____.

❽ The bride's father usually presents his daughter to her future husband. In other words he _____.

❾ The "event" which takes place in the church or registry office is known as _____.

❿ The party which is held afterwards is known as _____.

⓫ The holiday after the wedding is called _____.

2 the bridegroom / groom   **3** the bridesmaid   **4** the page boy
5 the best man   **6** the witnesses   **7** the guests
8 gives her away   **9** the ceremony   **10** the reception
11 the honeymoon

有些西方人會選擇宗教式的婚禮——在教堂裡結婚。還有一些人則選擇登記結婚，這種稱為 "civil ceremony"。在教堂中，負責婚禮儀式者是 "priest"（神父）或 "vicar"（教區牧師），而在登記結婚的登記處 "registry office"，儀式則是由 "registrar"（登記人）負責。

你現在對西方的婚禮是否更了解了呢？還有一點，"pageboys" 在婚禮中不太常見，只有少數新娘會選擇用男侍童。大部分在教堂結婚的新娘都會有至少一個 "bridesmaid"，新郎會有至少一個 "best man"（伴郎）；而在登記處登記的新娘則大多不會有伴娘，而是找 "witnesses"（證人）。

在教堂裡，新娘的爸爸會把女兒交給新郎。如果她沒有爸爸，則可以由哥哥或叔伯、舅舅等來完成。 在傳統的宗教婚禮上，"giving the bride away" 是個必經儀式。如果是普通的登記結婚，則不需要這個儀式。

婚禮宴客儀式可大可小，可以正式也可以不正式。許多人會選擇用 "buffet（自助餐）" 形式宴客，而不是正式的 "sit-down meal"，即圍桌而坐，由服務生上菜的形式。

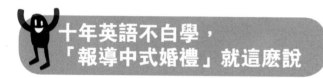

十年英語不白學，「報導中式婚禮」就這麼說

那麼中式婚禮和西式婚禮有什麼差別呢？在中式婚禮中，登記結婚的步驟和宴客比起來，反而沒有那麼重要，沒錯吧！

想像一下，如果你住的地方有英文報紙，而其中一名常在該報紙上寫文章的英文老師結婚了，他們把在報紙上刊登此事的任務交給了你，那你會怎麼寫呢？模仿前面看過的文章，在筆記本中寫寫看。完成並修改後，將它抄到作業本中。

在下表中可以找到和這次婚禮有關的資訊。

bride's name	Wang Yufeng
her occupation	teacher at No.4 Middle School
bridegroom's name	Chen Xigui
his occupation	engineer
home town	Longshan
place of official ceremony	Longshan registry office
time of ceremony	two weeks ago
place of reception	Golden King restaurant
time of reception	last week
type of reception	informal, sit-down lunch
No. of guests	45
bride's dress	red, silk
flowers	red roses
bride accompanied from her home by	her aunt, Zhang Xuqing
best man	Zhao Dali (groom's friend)
couple's first night	in their new home in the town centre

寫一篇描述此婚禮的文章。

請用以下的標題：

<u>Longshan Marriage</u>

Part 6——
社交英語無師自通，
道地的「有關婚禮問與答」該怎麼說？

十年英語不白學，
「想討論西方婚禮時」就這麼說

　　王玉鳳非常興奮，因為她要結婚了。她計劃在星期五的英文課堂上，和她的學生們聊聊西方的婚禮。這時，她發現她需要補充一些資訊，所以就請了她的英國朋友馬利恩（Marion）幫忙。

　　王玉鳳問了一些問題，而透過前面的內容，你應該已經能夠回答出不少她的問題了吧！把這些問題的答案寫在下面，不需要寫整句，只要意思表達清楚就夠了。第一題已經幫你寫好了！

回答問題。

❶ Where do official wedding ceremonies take place in Britain?

In a registry office or a church.

❷ Who take part in the wedding ceremony (apart from the general guests)?

❸ What does the bride usually wear?

❹ When is the wedding party / wedding reception held?

❺ Where is the reception held?

_____

❻ Is the reception formal or informal?

_____

❼ What do the newly married couple usually do after the reception?

_____

提示與解析

如果你的答案和我的範例答案不完全一樣也沒關係，只要重要的資訊表達清楚了即可。

❷ The bride, the groom, the bridesmaid, the best man, the witness, the bride's father.

❸ Usually a white dress.

❹ Immediately after the ceremony.

❺ Anywhere (at home, in a restaurant, in a hotel).

❻ Either (formal or informal).

❼ Go for their honeymoon.

　　王玉鳳問了她的朋友馬利恩一些問題，下面是她的回答。你是否能夠把這些答案與問題對應起來呢？請在下方空白處填入正確的問題。第一題已經為你做好了。請注意，問題的數量比答案多，在沒有用到的問題旁邊打叉。

從下一頁選擇正確的問題，寫在空格處。

1 What's a traditional wedding like in Britain? (h)
Well, a traditional wedding usually takes place in a church. The bride wears white and is given away by her father. There are usually two or three bridesmaids...

2 _____
In church weddings, the local vicar or priest and in registry offices, the registrar.

3 _____
They usually wear coloured dresses—the same colour: blue, pink, yellow or whatever the bride chooses.

4 _____
Well, his role is really to stay by the groom's side through the ceremony but he also takes care of the wedding ring—if there is one—and then, at the reception, he makes a speech.

5 _____
There are speeches and everyone eats, drinks and generally has a good time.

6 _____
No, there isn't. People eat a variety of things: hot meals, cold meals. It depends. But there is usually a special wedding cake.

7 _____
Again, it depends. Usually three or four hours.

a. What happens at the reception?

b. What does the vicar do?

c. What does the best man do?

d. Is there any special wedding food?

e. How long does the reception last?

f. How many guests are invited?

g. Who conducts the ceremony?

h. What's a traditional wedding like in Britain?

i. What do the bridesmaids wear?

j. What does the bridegroom wear?

提示與解析

2 Who conducts the ceremony? (g)

3 What do the bridesmaids wear? (i)

4 What does the best man do? (c)

5 What happens at the reception? (a)

6 Is there any special wedding food? (d)

7 How long does the reception last? (e)

沒有用到的問題： b, f, j

請注意第**1**題 What's a traditional wedding like in Britain? 這個句型。What is... like? 非常實用,可以拿來搭配很多的話題,例如:What's the weather like? What's Beijing like? What's the food like? What's your new teacher like?... 也可以用過去式來問： What was the film like? What was the exam like? What was your holiday like?... 此外,a 項 What happens at ...? 也是個很有用的句型。

十年英語不白學，「想討論中式婚禮時」就這麼說

現在請回頭看看前面兩個練習的所有問題，我們應該基本了解了如何詢問關於西方婚禮的事宜。那麼，換位思考一下，如果一個非華人朋友問你關於中式婚禮相關的問題，你會怎麼回答呢？

練習談論中式婚禮。

_____

_____

_____

_____

_____

提示與解析

1. Where does the official ceremony usually take place?
   At the local registry office.
2. Does anyone conduct the reception?
   Yes, usually there is a wedding host / hostess.
3. What do the bride and the groom wear?
   The bride usually wears a white dress or a traditional Chinese dress of red silk. The groom usually wears a suit.
4. What's the common type of reception?
   In most cases, it's a sit-down lunch.
5. Is there any witness at the wedding ceremony?
   Yes, and he / she usually makes a speech.

Part 7——
社交英語無師自通，
道地的「未來的願望、希望與計劃」該怎麼說？

接下來又有更多聽力測驗了，你準備好了嗎？

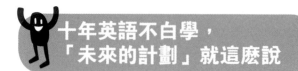

十年英語不白學，
「未來的計劃」就這麼說

　　莎倫與布萊爾太太（Mrs. Blair）兩人在購物中心巧遇，便聊起天來。她們聊得很開心，布萊爾太太回家後還和老公分享了她和莎倫的聊天內容。聽聽他們的對話，推斷看看布萊爾太太是如何和她老公開始對話的。完成以下的句子，使用兩個單字說明布萊爾太太與莎倫的聊天內容。

🔊 聽對話並完成以下句子。　　◀ *Track 006*

I met Sharon Appleby in town.　She told me all about her _____.

提示與解析

兩人聊天的主題是莎倫的 "future plans" 或 "marriage plans"，也就是這道題目的答案。

十年英語不白學，「想表達未來的人生規劃時」就這麼說

做完上個練習，我們已經很清楚莎倫和布萊爾太太聊天時是在討論莎倫未來的人生規劃。你應該已經知道，在英文中要討論「未來」時，有幾種不同的說法。再仔細聽一遍音檔，聽一聽莎倫人生規劃中的細節，將下面的句子補充完整。第一題已經為你做好了。

🔊 仔細聽音檔，將下面的句子補充完整。 ◀ *Track 006*

❶ We <u>are hoping to have</u> a summer wedding.

❷ It _____ a church wedding.

❸ Mum and Dad _____ the traditional thing and paying for the reception.

❹ We _____ inviting you and Mr. Blair, of course.

❺ I _____ an absolutely traditional wedding.

❻ I _____ looking at dresses soon.

❼ I _____ move in with him.

❽ We _____ to save up enough to move into a house after a couple of years.

❾ We _____ start a family just yet.

❿ We _____ wait three or four years.

⓫ He _____ four or five children.

⓬ I _____ if we only have one.

⓭ Are _____ a honeymoon?

⓮ We _____ find some sort of package tour to a peaceful Greek island.

兩人聊得很快，如果沒辦法完全寫下正確的詞句，也不用太沮喪！原句如下：

② It's going to be...

③ Mum and Dad are doing...

④ We'll be....

⑤ I'm planning...

⑥ I'm going to start...

⑦ I'm going to...

⑧ We're hoping...

⑨ We're not planning to...

⑩ We're going to...

⑪ He'd like to have...

⑫ I'll be happy...

⑬ Are you planning...

⑭ We're hoping to...

十年英語不白學，「未來的規劃和願望」就這麼說

現在我們來看看各種談論未來的句型：

ⓐ be going to（如：I'm going to move in with him.）

ⓑ be doing（如：Mum and Dad are doing the traditional thing...）

ⓒ will be / do if（如：I'll be happy if we only have one.）

ⓓ will be doing（如：We'll be inviting you...）

ⓔ be planning（如：I'm planning an absolutely traditional wedding. / We're not planning to start a family just yet.）

ⓕ would like（如：He'd like to have four or five children.）

ⓖ be hoping to（如：We're hoping to find some sort of package tour.）

以上七種談論未來的句型，共有六種不同的功能。要把語言的功能說清楚是很困難的，所以如果我的說明看起來有點複雜，也不要擔心！仔細看看上面的例子，判斷這些例子是屬於六類功能中的哪一類，並把答案寫在句子後面的橫線上。其中有的功能可以填入不只一項。

判斷上述的例子是屬於六類功能中的哪一類，並把答案寫在橫線上。

Functions	Example(s)
❶ Expressing a wish or a desire (which may or may not happen)	_____
❷ Expressing a plan that has been agreed / fixed (and which is likely to happen)	_____
❸ Expressing a plan which has been discussed but which has not been fixed / arranged so may or may not happen	_____
❹ Expressing plans that are still being made / still being discussed	_____
❺ Expressing a future state / event which depends on something else	_____
❻ Predicting / Expressing something that will happen but which has not been discussed	_____

提示與解析

❶ f "would like" 一般是用來表達願望或欲望。例如：I would like to move to a better flat.（我好想搬去一間更好的公寓。）在說這句話時，你自己也無法判斷你究竟會不會真能搬去一間更好的公寓，也就是說如果你已經決定好未來要搬去新公寓，甚至合約都簽了，就不能用這個說法。

再看個例子：Phil would like to have four or five children.（菲爾想要四個或五個孩子。）我們知道，菲爾自己一定也無法判斷他究竟會不會有四個或五個孩子，所以在這種情況下才會使用 "would like"。

② a, b, e 都可以用來表達「已經差不多非常確定」的計劃。例如：I'm moving in with him. 或 I'm going to move in with him. 都可以用來表示「我（確定）要搬去跟他一起住」。當然，他們還是有可能臨時忽然吵架什麼的，以致最後無法一起住，但至少在說話者「目前」的心理狀態中，是認定他們一定會住一起的。

③ g "be hoping to" 表示目前為止這個計劃還不完全確定。例如：We're hoping to have a summer wedding.（我們希望來場夏日婚禮。）說話者已經有初步的打算了，但還不完全確定能不能真的在那時候結婚。

④ e "be planning to" 表示目前為止這件事還在計劃中。"be planning to" 又比 "be hoping to" 更確定一些，因為已經在「規劃」了。

⑤ c 這種句子一般包含「條件」，例如： I'll be happy on the condition that we only have one child.（如果我們只有一個孩子，我就會開心。）這表示如果滿足了「只有一個孩子」的條件，說話者未來就會開心。

⑥ d 莎倫說了 "We'll be inviting you..."，而不是 "We're going to invite you..."，隱含的意思是她其實還沒完全確定要邀請誰，也沒跟任何人討論過要邀請布萊爾太太。她其實是邊講邊在腦中計劃的。

十年英語不白學，「慣用語」就這麼說

　　以下畫底線的句子都在對話裡出現過。勾選出最適合的選項，如果還有不太懂的地方，可以再聽一遍音檔。

🔊 在最恰當的選項旁邊打勾。　◀ *Track 006*

❶ She's <u>over the moon</u> about your news.
　a. very far away　b. very happy
　c. very worried　d. very upset

❷ He's quite happy to <u>let me have my own way</u>.
　a. to allow me to choose what I want
　b. to allow me to go there alone
　c. to allow me to use a map
　d. to allow me to do it alone

❸ ... but <u>there's no rush</u>.
　a. there's no rent to pay　　b. we have no worries
　c. we don't have to hurry　d. we don't have any furniture

❹ We're hoping to find some sort of <u>package tour</u>.
　a. wedding present
　b. a completely planned holiday
　c. a shopping trip
　d. a camping holiday

❺ ... but don't let me <u>keep you</u>.
　a. take care of you　　b. give you money
　c. delay you　　　　　d. stop you from travelling

從這段對話中，我們可以判斷莎倫是個年輕女子。那布萊爾太太呢？她年紀不小了，沒錯吧！她用了很多俚語，語氣也顯得比較老氣。這個練習中出現的片語就是一些慣用的俚語說法。

❶ b "over the moon" 是「非常開心」的意思。不過，這個俚語知道就好，其實用 "very happy" 表達開心就可以了。

❷ a

❸ c

❹ b 也就是我們熟悉的跟團旅行，由旅行社把一切安排好，包括交通、住宿、飲食、導遊等。

❺ c

Part 8——
社交英語無師自通，
道地的「我的願望、希望與計劃」該怎麼寫？

你的最後一個作業，就是回頭復習整個單元。你現在是否能夠充滿信心地談論各種人際關係了呢？

學完這一單元，你就可以：

☐ 問一些比較私人的問題。

☐ 問一些關於各種人際關係的問題。

☐ 描述各種人際關係。

☐ 表達惋惜之意。

☐ 描述結婚與婚禮的傳統習俗。

☐ 描述未來的願望、希望與計劃等。

看看之前的練習中提到的所有表示願望、希望與計劃的說法。仔細聽音檔中的每一句話，注意發音與語調，並進行跟讀。接下來想想自己的未來，使用各種句型來表達自己的願望、希望與計劃。大聲朗讀，然後將自己所朗讀的句子錄下來。

記下你的願望、希望與計劃。

請使用以下標題：

<u>Wishes, Hopes and Plans</u>

第二單元總復習

十年英語不白學，
「想談論一段成功的婚姻時」就這麼說

接下來你會聽到一段電臺節目，內容是一對夫婦接受訪談，談論他們成功的婚姻。

◀ *Track 007*

 聽弗蘭克（**Frank**）與莉莉（**Lily**）的訪談，改正以下句子中的錯誤。

❶ Frank and Lily have just celebrated their Golden Wedding Anniversary.

❷ They met 38 years ago at a disco.

❸ Frank was Lily's dancing partner from the beginning.

❹ He was a very bad dancer then.

❺ Frank asked Lily to marry him three years later.

❻ Lily wanted Frank to finish his exams first and get a career.

❼ They have two children, a daughter and a son.

❽ Both their children are now married with a child.

❾ Lily thinks part of their success is due to Frank's admiration of her.

❿ They only recently started to share the housework duties.

⓫ Lily does most of the cooking.

⓬ Frank is Financial Director of a big company.

⓭ Lily works just round the corner.

⓮ If they don't feel like cooking, they eat at their daughter's house.

⓯ They still go dancing, but not very regularly.

⓰ When they dance, they like to talk about work.

提示與解析

1. Frank and Lily have just celebrated their Silver Wedding Anniversary.
2. They met 28 years ago at a dancing school.
3. Frank was Lily's friend Joan's dancing partner at the beginning.
4. He was a good dancer then.
5. Frank asked Lily to marry him two years later.
6. Lily wanted to finish her exams first and get a career.
7. They have two children, two daughters.
8. Their elder daughter is now married with a child.
9. Lily thinks part of their success is due to Frank's respect for her.
10. They have always shared the housework duties.
11. Frank does most of the cooking.
12. Lily is Financial Director of a big company.
13. Frank works just round the corner.
14. If they don't feel like cooking, they eat out or get a take-away.
15. They still go dancing every Saturday evening.
16. When they dance, they like to forget about work.

MP3音檔內容完整看

　　若是聽完音檔還是沒把握，建議可搭配本部份學習，不熟的語彙要查辭典並作筆記，方能加深英文記憶。

Part 1: Track 004　（請配合083頁及音檔使用）

❶ I hope you don't mind me asking but are you married?

❷ Forgive me for asking but do you have a boyfriend?

❸ Excuse my curiosity but do you have any children?

❹ I hope you don't mind me asking but how long have you been married?

❺ Forgive me for asking but how long have you known your wife?

❻ Excuse my curiosity but where did you meet your husband?

❼ I hope you don't mind me asking but are you going out with anybody?

❽ Forgive me for asking but when are you getting married?

❾ Excuse my curiosity but how old were you when you got married?

Part 4: Track 005　（請配合105、106、110、111頁及音檔使用）

Sharon: Hey, Ruth, thanks for showing such interest in all my plans and so on. You're being great!

Ruth: Oh, I'm enjoying all the excitement... still trying to make up for the fact that my own wedding was so boring, I suppose.

Sharon: You've never talked much about your wedding... or your marriage, have you? I suppose I just think of you as a divorced woman and forget that you were once a bride.

Ruth: Yes, but there was no white dress or expensive reception for me. And yet, I would have loved a big wedding.

Sharon: So were you married in a registry office? You don't mind me asking, do you?

Ruth:	No, of course I don't mind you asking and, yes, I was married in a registry office—in an ugly old building in north London... a ten-minute ceremony that was totally lacking in romance.
Sharon:	But registry office weddings can be nice; I've been to some good ones with lots of guests and lots of fun.
Ruth:	Well, we didn't have lots of guests. There were only four people apart from me and my husband to be. Four friends, including our two witnesses.
Sharon:	So, forgive me for asking, but weren't your parents there?
Ruth:	No, no parents. And I wore a very simple cream dress—loose fitting to hide the fact that I was pregnant. But, of course, everyone knew anyway!
Sharon:	Ah! I'd often wondered if you "had to be married" as they say. You're so young to have a 16-year-old daughter.
Ruth:	Yes, in fact I was younger than Rose when I started going out with Frankie. Only 15, in fact. Far too young. And 17 when I got married. Far too young. I wish I hadn't been so silly.
Sharon:	Don't be so hard on yourself. You must have loved your ex-husband. Excuse my curiosity, but what's his name?
Ruth:	Frankie. We all used to call him "Fab Frankie" because we thought he was fabulous. He was so handsome... and he completely swept me off my feet when we first met at a party. Now, I just wish I'd never met him! He treated the whole marriage as a joke. And I think I knew, even before the wedding, that he would make a terrible husband and father. I wish I'd told him to "get lost" then!
Sharon:	Oh, you poor thing. Did you tell anyone how you felt?
Ruth:	No, I just pretended I was happy.
Sharon:	You must have been terrified!
Ruth:	Yes, I was, you're right. All my friends were making plans to go to college and I was just getting ready for the baby. She was born five months after the wedding and Frankie left me a month later.

Sharon: Really? I hadn't realised. Oh, Ruth, I'm so sorry. I shouldn't have asked you to talk about all this.

Ruth: Oh, that's fine. I can laugh about it now. My life's been quite good really. Of course, I've made lots of mistakes and there are a million things I wish I'd done... university, travel, a good job and so on. But, I've really enjoyed being a mother. You've seen how close Rose and I are. And I like this job.

Sharon: Yes... I've never thought of you as a sad person.

Ruth: No, in fact, funnily enough, that's what attracted Frankie to me in the first place. He always called me "Miss Cheerful". And, you know, my parents were fantastic. I mean, they had such high hopes for me because I used to do very well at school. But they never added to my problems by making me feel guilty. They were so kind. Otherwise things could definitely have been worse.

Sharon: Oh, dear. I feel almost tearful.

Ruth: Well, don't. I don't even feel sorry for myself these days, so there's no need for you to feel sorry for me.

Part 7: Track 006   （請配合128、129、133頁及音檔使用）

Mrs. Blair: Sharon! Hello. I gather congratulations are in order. I saw your mum yesterday and she's over the moon about your news. Congratulations! When will the happy day be?

Sharon: Well, we're hoping to have a summer wedding—probably around the end of June or the beginning of July. But we have to go and see the vicar to fix an exact date.

Mrs. Blair: So, it's going to be a church wedding. I am glad. It would be a pity if you were married in a registry office. Your mum would be disappointed... After all, it's a very special day in one's life... and most of us only do it once!

Sharon: Yes, I agree. Phil wouldn't have minded a registry office but he's quite happy to let me have my own way! And, since Mum and Dad are doing the traditional thing and paying for the reception, he's leaving it entirely up to me to draw up the guest list. We'll be inviting you and Mr. Blair, of course.

Mrs. Blair: Oh, how lovely. Thank you. And, er, are you going to wear white?

Sharon: Definitely. I'm planning an absolutely traditional wedding. As you say, I'm only planning to do this once in my life! I'm going to start looking at dresses soon. I'm really excited about it.

Mrs. Blair: Well, it is a very exciting time... planning the beginning of your whole future! Where are you going to live?

Sharon: Well, Phil already has a flat in town so I'm going to move in with him and we'll start our married life there... and then, we're hoping to save up enough to move into a house after a couple of years... but there's no rush. His flat's quite nice.

Mrs. Blair: That's good. But is there enough space for children there?

Sharon: Oh, Mrs. Blair, you are funny! We're not planning to start a family just yet. We're going to wait three or four years. There's plenty of time for that.

Mrs. Blair: Well, that depends how many children you want.

Sharon: Yes, I suppose it does. Phil loves kids... and he's from a big family himself. He was saying the other day that he'd like to have four or five children... but I'll be happy if we only have one, I think. We'll probably compromise and have two or three.

Mrs. Blair: Oh, I do envy you. Are you planning a honeymoon?

Sharon: Well. Yes... but I'm not sure where. We're hoping to find some sort of package tour to a peaceful Greek island.

Mrs. Blair: Oh, Greece. How wonderful! You know, I've never been abroad.

Sharon: Well, you should go. You could afford it.

Mrs. Blair: I would go all over the world if I were your age... but don't let me keep you. I'm sure you have lots to do... a busy working girl... soon to be a busy working wife! I'm so happy about your news. It's been lovely talking to you.

Sharon: Yes, I've enjoyed seeing you. I won't forget your invitation.

Mrs. Blair: You'd better not! I'd never forgive you if you did... I've known you all your life so I must see you get married.

Sharon: You will, you will. Bye-bye.

Mrs. Blair: Bye dear. Look after yourself... Oh, dear, I didn't see her engagement ring... Sharon... Sharon... Oh, dear, she's gone.

 **第二單元總復習: Track 007** （請配合137頁及音檔使用）

A Successful Marriage

Interviewer: On today's programme we're looking at what makes a marriage successful. In the studio, we have several couples who have been happily married for more than 20 years. We're going to ask them to explain to us the secret of their success. Now the first couple we're going to meet are Frank and Lily Spencer from Colchester. Lily, shall we start with you?

Lily: Certainly.

Interviewer: How long have you and Frank been married?

Lily: Twenty-five years.

Interviewer: Oh, congratulations! How did you celebrate your Silver Wedding Anniversary?

Lily: Our children organised a lovely party—just family and close friends.

Interviewer: Hmm... Could you tell us how you and Frank met?

Lily:	Yes, we met 28 years ago at a dancing school. You see, I wanted to learn ballroom dancing, and I went to this school in the evenings with my friend Joan. We didn't have dancing partners, so the dancing instructor found us two single men to dance with.
Interviewer:	So, Frank was your dancing partner?
Lily:	Oh, no. Frank was Joan's partner. My partner was terrible—he seemed to have two left feet and my toes were so sore after dancing with him! I noticed Joan's partner was a good dancer, so when she left and went to work in London, I asked Frank if he would be my partner and he agreed.
Interviewer:	So, was it love at first sight, Frank?
Frank:	Well, not really. We met once a week at the dancing school for one year. And then we gradually began to realise how much we looked forwards to it each week. And then it dawned on us that we could see more of each other, so we started going out to the cinema, and had picnics together at weekends and so on.
Interviewer:	So when did you pop the question?
Frank:	Oh, I asked Lily to marry me after two years. She agreed, but asked me to wait until she'd finished her accountancy exams.
Lily:	Yes, I wanted to make sure I was fully qualified and had a career before I started having children. Otherwise, I thought, I might never have the chance.
Interviewer:	Well, you had two children eventually.
Lily:	Yes, two girls... we're a very close family. Our daughters both still live in Colchester, so we see them every week. The elder one is married and she has just had a son herself.
Interviewer:	Ah, so you're grandparents!
Frank:	Yes, we are and we love it. We hope there'll be more grandchildren on the way soon.
Interviewer:	So, what is the secret of your success?

Lily:	Well, I think for me, it's the fact that Frank has always respected me. He's supported me in my career. I took a few years off to have the children and Frank always rushed home to help me... and he was always happy to do his share of the duties, so that I could go back to work.
Interviewer:	Have you always shared the housework and looked after the children?
Frank:	Oh, yes. Well, I believe a two-way thing. I mean, why should my wife do two jobs? It's not fair to her to work all day at the office and then come home and clean the house and make the dinner.
Interviewer:	So, you share the cooking duties too?
Frank:	Well, actually, I do most of the cooking, as I usually get home earlier. You see, Lily is now Financial Director of a big company and that keeps her at work often till late in the evening. She often comes home exhausted.
Interviewer:	And what do you do for a living, Frank?
Frank:	I'm a dentist. My surgery finishes at 5:30 usually, and it's just round the corner, so I'm usually back by six. If I'm not too tired, I'll cook, or if we're both too tired we'll go out and eat, or get a take-away. You see, we're very flexible. We don't have strict rules.
Interviewer:	Is there anything else that has made your marriage a success?
Lily:	Oh, yes, definitely! We have never given up dancing. We go dancing every Saturday night and that's our time for relaxing together, forgetting work and just having fun!
Frank:	Yes, we still have a lot of fun together.
Interviewer:	Well, thank you very much, Frank and Lily. Now our next couple... (fade out)

Unit 1

Unit 2

生活與人際關係 Life and Relationships

Unit 3 Unit 4

NOTE

NOTE

Unit 3 健康 Health

Unit 3 健康

Health

　　隨著全球現代化、工業化、資訊化、都市化發展的加快，人們為了追求更好的生活品質，承受著巨大的壓力。醫學研究報告顯示，大約有20%至30%的人每天因工作或生活壓力，形成熬夜及不規律的飲食習慣，而這些不良習慣引發了一系列的症狀。人們在享受物質生活的同時，也付出著身心健康的代價。讓我們一起來關注自身及身邊親朋好友的健康狀況，學習如何應對壓力造成的負面影響，並使你的英語口語更加流利。

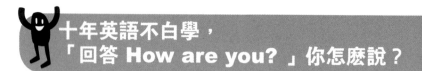

十年英語不白學，「回答 How are you?」你怎麼說？

　　當別人問你 "How are you?" 的時候，可以根據自身情況來回答。下面這些句子都是合適的回答。請將這些說法按照身體不同的狀態進行分類。

　　請將這些說法分別填入表格中。第一題已經為你做好了！

ⓐ I feel dreadful.

ⓑ I'm worn out.

ⓒ I'm all right.

ⓓ I'm fine.

ⓔ I'm not too bad.

ⓕ I'm a bit under the weather.

ⓖ I'm not very well.

ⓗ I feel marvellous.

ⓘ I feel really bad.

ⓙ I'm sick.

ⓚ I feel rather unwell.

ⓛ I'm very well.

ⓜ I think I must be coming down with something.

① in excellent health	h. I feel marvellous.
② in good / average health	
③ with a slight problem	
④ definitely sick	

提示與解析

如果你的答案和我的解答不完全一樣，也不用太擔心，因為這四種類型的回答之間本來就沒有很明確的界限，甚至有時候需要搭配說話者的聲調和表情，才能判斷對方到底是想表達什麼。舉例來說，如果你問對方 "How are you?"，對方用痛苦的表情回答 "Very well."，那顯然不能把它歸在第一類。一般而言，我們可以推斷說 "I feel marvellous."（我感覺超級好。）或 "I'm very well."（我非常好。）的人應該屬於第1類（in excellent health）。第2類（in good / average health）可能包含 ⓒ 、ⓓ 以及ⓔ 。第3類（with a slight problem）可能包含ⓑ 、ⓕ 、ⓜ ，也可能會包含ⓔ 和ⓖ 、ⓚ 。至於第4類（definitely sick）則可能回答ⓐ 、ⓘ 、ⓙ 或ⓚ ，ⓖ 也可能算數，雖然只說 "I'm not very well."（我有點不太好。）聽起來不嚴重，但說話者也有可能只是沒有表現出來。

答案：
① → ⓗ ⓛ
② → ⓒ ⓓ（ⓔ 也可）
③ → ⓑ ⓕ ⓜ（ⓔ ⓖ ⓚ 也可）
④ → ⓐ ⓘ ⓙ（ⓖ ⓚ 也可）

社交英語無師自通，你一定還想知道更多！

其實，"How are you?" 這個問題通常是一種禮貌性的問法，問問題的人不是期待對方回答具體怎樣，很多時候，這是開啓一段對話的自然的方式。一般而言，只要回答 "I'm fine, thank you." 就可以了，只有當你很確定對方真的很想知道你好不好時，才需要做詳細的回答。

Part 1——
社交英語無師自通，
道地的「有關健康的問答」該怎麼說？

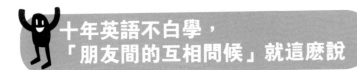

**十年英語不白學，
「朋友間的互相問候」就這麼說**

聽音檔中的對話，試著推斷兩人之間的關係，並判斷他們即將談論的主題。請從四個選項中勾選出最合適的答案。聽到 "I'm sure you are not in a fit state to do any work." 時，請先把音檔暫停。

🔊) 聽音檔，勾選出最合適的選項。　◀*Track 008*

❶ The relationship between the two speakers is _____.
   a. teacher and student
   b. doctor and patient
   c. friends
   d. boss and employee

❷ The speakers are _____.
   a. describing visits to the doctor
   b. talking about hospitals
   c. discussing keeping fit
   d. talking about a health problem

提示與解析

由對話的前幾句，我們就可以判斷出說話的兩人應該是很好的朋友，而男性泰瑞（Terry）大概會給生病中的女性杜薇一點建議。這個對話聽起來很友善吧！一般而言，不熟的人不會具體聊身體健康方面的事，而且像 "You don't look too good."（你看起來不怎麼好。）和 "You poor thing."（可憐的人。）這種句子一般只有好朋友之間在非正式場合才會用。因此，正確答案為：
❶ c　❷ d

十年英語不白學，「想詢問對方身體狀況時」就這麼說

你應該已經知道一些詢問別人身體狀況的不同方式了。比如剛才音檔中對話的開始部分 "Hi, Du Wei. What's wrong with you? You don't look too good." 就是個很典型的例子。以下列出一些其他的表達方式，請從方框中選出合適的單字或片語填入句中。有些單字或片語可以多次使用，個別題目的答案並非唯一。第一題已經為你做好了！

完成句子。

wrong	matter	problem	all right	up

❶ Hi, John. What's the _matter_ with you? You look dreadful.

❷ Hello, Gao. What's _____ with you? You look rather pale.

❸ Natalie, are you _____? You look as if you have a cold.

❹ Hi, Zhu. You don't look too good. Is there something _____?

❺ Hello, Cathy. You're not looking very well. What's the _____?

提示與解析

如上面所說，一個空白有可能不只一個答案。

❷ wrong / up　❸ all right　❹ wrong　❺ matter / problem

社交英語無師自通，你一定還想知道更多！

請注意這些不同的說法：

◆ What's **the** matter (with you)?
◆ What's **the** problem (with you)?
◆ What's wrong (with you)?
◆ What's up (with you)?

前兩種表達方式需要用到定冠詞 "the"，後面兩種則不需要。
"What's up (with you)?" 是種不太正式的問法，年輕人使用較多。

十年英語不白學，「描述症狀」就這麼說

　　在聽Track 008的對話時，你聽出杜薇的健康問題了嗎？原來她感冒了，而且還是重感冒。從兩人的談話中，我們可以聽出杜薇究竟有哪些症狀，可以判斷出她感覺如何、看起來怎樣。杜薇也提到自己採取了哪些措施幫助身體康復。現在請再聽一遍音檔，根據音檔內容判斷下面句子的對錯，在正確的句子後打勾，不正確的句子後打叉，並在橫線上寫出正確的句子。第一題已經為你做好了。

🔊 聽音檔，判斷句子對錯。請在正確的句子打勾，不正確的句子打叉，並在橫線上寫出正確的句子。　◀ *Track 008*

❶ Du Wei's lips are sore. (X)

　 Du Wei's eyes are sore.

❷ She feels all stuffed up and thick-headed. (　)

❸ Her nose looks sore. (　　)

_____

❹ She feels marvellous. (　　)

_____

❺ She can't think straight. (　　)

_____

❻ She's very strong. (　　)

_____

❼ She's not in a fit state to do any work. (　　)

_____

❽ She doesn't feel like doing anything except sleeping. (　　)

_____

❾ She is taking some medicine. (　　)

_____

❿ She is eating lots. (　　)

_____

⓫ She's taking vitamin C. (　　)

_____

提示與解析

正確的句子：**❷**,**❸**,**❺**,**❼**,**❽**,**⓫**
❹ 應改為：She feels awful.
❻ 應改為：She's very weak.
❾ 應改為：She isn't taking any medicine.
❿ 應改為：She's drinking lots.

十年英語不白學，「描述症狀及治療方式」就這麼說

　　再讀一遍上面練習中的句子，請判斷哪些句子描述的是症狀，哪些描述的是針對症狀的治療方式。把正確的句子編號寫在下方對應的表格中。

把正確的句子編號填寫到適當的位置。

Sentences describing Du Wei's symptoms:	
Sentences describing Du Wei's treatment:	

提示與解析

描述症狀（symptoms）：❶, ❷, ❸, ❹, ❺, ❻, ❼, ❽
描述治療方式（treatment）：❾, ❿, ⓫

十年英語不白學，「表達關心」就這麼說

　　泰瑞似乎很擔心杜薇，提供了不少建議。再聽一遍對話，完成以下句子。

🔊 聽音檔，在橫線上填入適當的單字。　◀ *Track 008*

❶ You _____ _____ at home, in bed.

② Why _____ _____ go home?

③ It _____ _____ _____ better if you went home and went to bed.

④ Have _____ _____ Vitese?

⑤ You really _____ _____ _____ of yourself.

提示與解析

你可能會發現，泰瑞非常希望杜薇趕快回家睡覺，因為光這件事他就說了三次，還換了三個不同的說法。這個練習的答案是：

① You <u>should</u> <u>be</u> at home, in bed.

② Why <u>don't</u> <u>you</u> go home?

③ It <u>would</u> <u>be</u> <u>much</u> better if you went home and went to bed.

④ Have <u>you</u> <u>tried</u> Vitese?

⑤ You really <u>should</u> <u>take</u> <u>care</u> of yourself.

十年英語不白學，「描述藥品特性」就這麼說

泰瑞建議杜薇試一試 "Vitese"。這是什麼藥呢？仔細聽聽他是怎樣詳細描述這種藥品的，並完成以下表格。

🔊 聽音檔，完成表格。　◀Track 008

Name	Vitese
Treatment for	
Form (liquid, tablet, powder)	
Contents	

Instructions	
Available from	

提示與解析

The medicine that Terry recommends to Du Wei is called Vitese. It made him feel better when he had an awful cold. It is a powder that should be mixed with hot water. It has a lot of vitamin C in it, but contains aspirin or paracetemol as well. This medicine can be bought in any chemist's.

（泰瑞推薦給杜薇的藥品叫 "Vitese"，可以有效治療感冒，這種藥是粉狀的，要和熱水混著一起喝。裡面含有很多維生素C，但也含有阿斯匹林和解熱鎮痛劑。這種藥品在任何藥房都買得到。）

社交英語無師自通，你一定還想知道更多！

　　從上面這段話中我們能看到如何詳細描述藥品。同樣的描述方式，後面的練習中還會出現。

　　順便說明一下，"chemist's" 指的是一種英國的藥房，銷售藥品與保健用品。請注意，只有加 "'s" 才指藥房。如果沒有 "'s"，"chemist" 是指藥劑師。在美國，藥房則稱為 "pharmacy"，藥劑師叫做 "pharmacist"（英式英語中也可以使用這個單字）。

十年英語不白學，「表達建議」就這麼說

為別人提供建議時，有很多句型可以使用，究竟該使用哪個句型則必須視以下兩點而定：

a) 說話的對象
b) 建議的內容

在我們之前聽的音檔中，泰瑞給予建議時，使用的都是很直接的句型：

You should be at home...
Why don't you go home?
Have you tried Vitese?
You really should take care of yourself.

他甚至還說：*Don't go to the library. That's an order.*

像這樣直接的句型，通常只有很熟的朋友之間才會用。一般而言，我們不會給予不熟的人這樣直接的建議。

如果想要在更正式的場合提供建議，你可以嘗試使用下面方框中的句型。練習說一說方框中的句子。

拒當英文句點王，換你練習開口說說看！

Formal contexts （正式情境）
a. I was wondering if you'd thought of (having an operation)?
b. Don't you think it might be a good idea to (ride your bicycle to go to work rather than take the bus)?

Semi-formal contexts （半正式情境）

c. I think it might be a good idea to (have a short holiday on the beach).

d. I think you could (take some vitamin C every day).

e. Have you thought of (going out and getting some fresh air once in a while)?

f. If I were you, I'd (smoke less).

g. My advice would be (drinking more water and eating more vegetables).

h. If you followed my advice, you'd (go home and stay in bed for two days).

i. I'd advise you (to cut the fat off the meat).

j. I'd say (a little exercise would do you no harm).

Informal contexts （非正式情境）

k. Why don't you (go dancing instead of playing cards)?

l. You'd better (go on a diet).

m. You should (take more exercise).

n. You mustn't (drink that much).

十年英語不白學，「針對不同需求提出適合的建議」就這麼說

　　下面列出的這些人都需要建議。你是否能向他們提供一些建議呢？別忘了，要針對不同的對象，選擇最適合的句型。將你的建議寫在每道題下方的橫線上，第一題已經為你做好了！

給以下這些人一些建議。

1 An American professor whom you've met once or twice is visiting your school. He looks much paler than usual and is sweating a lot.

Don't you think it might be a good idea to see a doctor?

2 Your Australian friend is rather overweight. He's depressed because he doesn't have a girlfriend and girls just don't seem to be interested in him.

3 A Russian colleague who arrived at your workplace recently has just told you that she has a terrible headache.

4 The father of a British friend is visiting your town. He smokes all the time and has a terrible cough.

5 A British friend has a health problem. The doctors have suggested that she either have an operation or use drugs to control the situation.

6 The foreign teacher at your workplace is a good friend of yours. You notice that she is pale and has dark rings under her eyes. You know she's been taking medicine for an upset stomach for the last few days but doesn't seem to be getting any better.

7 The British person sitting beside you on a train journey has just commented that he feels sick and dizzy.

如前面所說，我們在給予建議的時候，必須視「說話的對象」和「建議的內容」來決定該使用怎樣的句型，所以在回答這些問題時也要特別注意這兩點。你給的建議可能和參考答案不完全一樣，這並沒有關係，這裡主要列出應該選擇用怎樣的句型來提供建議。

② 選擇半正式或非正式句型，如：
Have you thought of **going on a diet?**
Why don't you **do some exercise?**

③ 選擇半正式句型，如：
My advice would be **to go home and go to bed.**
I think it might be a good idea to **take an aspirin.**

④ 選擇正式的句型，如：
I was wondering if you'd thought of **giving up smoking?**
Don't you think it might be a good idea to **smoke less?**

⑤ 選擇半正式句型（雖然這個人是你朋友，但因為這個情境比較嚴肅，不適合用非正式句型）。如：
If I were you, I'd **have the operation.**
If you followed my advice, you'd **take drugs rather than have an operation.**

⑥ 選擇非正式句型，如：
Why don't you **go to a doctor?**
You should **stop taking that medicine.**

⑦ 選擇正式句型，如：
Don't you think it might be a good idea to **open the window?**
I was wondering if you'd thought of **having a drink?**

　　我們知道泰瑞和杜薇是好朋友。因此，杜薇才能直接說她很不舒服，而泰瑞也才能非常直接地給予意見。在對話結束時，杜薇說自己 "too weak to argue"，也同意馬上去藥房。她還跟泰瑞說："You sound like an old woman." 杜薇當然是在開玩笑，而且相信她對泰瑞的幫助是心懷感激的。我們可以對親近的朋友或家人說 "You sound like..."，這是一種開玩笑的方式。請閱讀以下描述，選擇方框中的片語完成 "You sound like..." 的句子，並把句子寫在橫線上。第一題已經為你做好了！

 選用方框中的片語完成句子。

a banker	*a politician*	*a photographer*	*my mother*
a poet	*a doctor*	*an army officer*	*a football hooligan*

❶ Frank is talking about ways of making extra money and giving you lots of (unasked for) advice on spending and saving.

(You say:) *You sound like a banker.*

❷ Your friend Linda keeps asking how you are, what you've eaten, how much sleep you had, etc.

(You say:) _____

❸ Vicky loves giving advice and recommending which medicine to take.

(You say:) _____

❹ John is talking about his ideas for solving the world's problems.

(You say:) _____

⑤ Ann is rather sentimental, and she often uses flowery or rhyming words to express her ideas.

(You say:) _____

⑥ Pete is shouting and screaming and making a lot of noise.

(You say:) _____

⑦ Jacob is always giving orders and telling people what to do.

(You say:) _____

⑧ Whenever you want to take a picture, your mother would tell you how to choose the angle, how to adjust focus, and how to catch the right moment, etc.

(You say:) _____

提示與解析

請記得，像這種開玩笑用的口語句子如果只寫就沒意思了，一定要大聲說出來才行！聽聽看音檔中杜薇說 "You sound like an old woman." 時的口氣並模仿一下。

答案：

❷ You sound like my mother.
❸ ... a doctor.
❹ ... a politician.
❺ ... a poet.
❻ ... a football hooligan.
❼ ... an army officer.
❽ ... a photographer.

在剛剛聽到的對話中，出現了一些很實用的說法，列舉如下。這些說法的含義都列在了下面的方框中，請選出最合適的選項和句子匹配。如果碰到不太確定的情況，可以再聽一遍音檔，根據上下文進行推理。將最適當的選項的字母寫在句子後面的橫線上。第一題已經為你做好了！

🔊)) 聽音檔，從方框中選出最合適的解釋和句子進行匹配。◀┋ *Track 008*

❶ You're not in a fit state to do any work.　　　　　　　n

❷ Are you taking anything?　　　　　　　＿＿＿

❸ What did you say it was called?　　　　　＿＿＿

❹ I'd really recommend it.　　　　　　　　＿＿＿

❺ It made me feel better after just a couple of doses.　＿＿＿

❻ Don't be a martyr.　　　　　　　　　　＿＿＿

❼ Don't overdo the tender loving care.　　　＿＿＿

❽ I don't like people making a fuss when I'm ill .　＿＿＿

---

a. What did you say your name was?

b. Don't fall in love with me.

c. I think it's very good.

d. My health improved after I'd taken it twice.

e. Don't suffer unnecessarily.

f. You don't get enough exercise.

g. Tell me the name again, please.

h. I had the illness a couple of times.

i. Don't be too kind to me.

j. I don't like people who are often sick.

k. Are you taking any medicine?

l. Are you carrying any luggage?

m. I feel uncomfortable when people give me too much attention.

n. You're not well enough to study now.

提示與解析

這些都是非正式的說法，很口語化。尤其是第三題，要用來搞清楚一個東西到底叫什麼名字時，這句可是非常實用的。

答案：**2** k **3** g **4** c **5** d **6** e **7** i **8** m

Part 2──
社交英語無師自通，
道地的「有關健康的案例」該怎麼說？

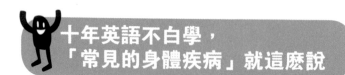

**十年英語不白學，
「常見的身體疾病」就這麼說**

你應該已經知道一些常見的健康問題用英文怎麼說了吧。在以下空白處寫下一些你所知道的疾病或健康問題。我已經為你寫好一個例子了！

寫下一些你所知道的疾病或健康問題。

a headache

提示與解析

下面列出的是一些健康問題。如果你沒有全部寫出來也沒關係，在本單元接下來的部分中，我們還會學到很多健康問題的說法。

a headache（頭痛），a cold（感冒），a cough（咳嗽），a sore throat（喉嚨痛），a fever（發燒），flu（流行性感冒），a toothache（牙痛），a backache（背痛），a stomach ache（肚子痛），an upset stomach（腸胃不適），an earache（耳朵痛），a stiff neck（脖子僵硬），tonsillitis（扁桃腺炎）

十年英語不白學，「根據症狀判斷出疾病問題時」就這麼說

　　健康出問題，身體就會產生一些特殊反應。例如感冒發燒時我們可能覺得渾身發熱，什麼都不想吃。在前面的對話中，杜薇就說她因感冒而覺得 "all stuffed up and thick-headed"（渾身發脹、頭暈），除了睡覺什麼也不想做。這些就是 "symptoms"（症狀）。你能將以下方框中的「症狀」與「健康問題」對應起來嗎？第一題已經為你做好了。在空白處寫下句子，描述導致症狀產生的相應健康問題。可以使用以下句型：

He / She probably has...

The Problems:

a hangover	*indigestion*	*food poisoning*	*a fever*
a fever measles	*tonsillitis*	*flu (influenza)*	

 寫下導致症狀產生的相應的健康問題。

❶ Tim has been vomiting all night. He is sick again immediately after breakfast and can't keep anything down. He's very pale and feels awful.

He probably has food poisoning.

❷ Liu feels very weak and dizzy. He aches all over and can't stop shivering.

(He) _____.

❸ Mei Ling can't swallow. Her neck glands are swollen. She feels very weak.

(She) _____.

❹ Ning Ning developed a cold a few days ago, then she started to cough and now she has a rash—small spots—all over her body. She feels uncomfortable and has a high temperature.

(She) _____.

❺ Stan went to a party last night and drank quite a lot of beer and wine. This morning he feels dreadful. He has a headache and feels sick and dizzy.

(He) _____.

❻ Han keeps feeling very hot and then very cold. His face changes from being red and "flushed" to quite pale. He took his temperature and found it was 40°C.

(He) _____.

❼ George is visiting friends in France. He has begun to feel unwell. His stomach is bloated and is quite painful. He feels full of gas.

(He) _____.

提示與解析

答案：

❷ He probably has flu.

❸ She probably has tonsillitis.

❹ She probably has a fever measles.

❺ He probably has a hangover.

❻ He probably has a fever.

❼ He probably has indigestion.

十年英語不白學，
「有關健康問題的文章標題」就這麼說

　　以下的兩篇文章都是個人對疾病狀況的描述。請快速瀏覽一遍，從以下選項中為這些文章選出適當的標題寫在相應的橫線上。

ⓐ An Unpleasant Experience

ⓑ A Terrible Accident

ⓒ My Medical History

ⓓ A Continuing Problem

ⓔ An Upset Stomach

 為以下的文章選擇適當的標題。

TEXT 1 _____

(1) I've never really had any major health problems but something rather unpleasant happened to me about three years ago. (2) I'd been

feeling uncomfortable for a couple of days, as if I might be coming down with flu. (3) Then I woke up one morning and felt strange. (4) The left side of my face felt numb but I thought that feeling would soon disappear. (5) Then I went to the bathroom to brush my teeth and looked in the mirror. (6) I was horrified. (7) I discovered that the whole of the left side of my face was paralysed. (8) There was no movement there at all. (9) My eyes couldn't close and the left side of my mouth stayed still when I tried to smile. (10) I looked so ugly but I didn't feel ill. (11) I didn't know what to do and still kept hoping that the problem would go away. (12) An hour later, I realised there was no improvement so I went to see a doctor. (13) He immediately recognised the problem. (14) He told me that I had something called Bell's Palsy. (15) He said that it was a fairly common problem but that not very much was known about it. (16) Apparently, it may be caused by a virus but medical experts do not fully understand it. (17) The doctor explained that recovery rates varied but that it would probably take about six weeks for my face to return normal. (18) He warned me that some people never recovered and others only partially recovered so I was rather worried. (19) He prescribed medication and arranged for me to visit the hospital every day to have therapy on my face. (20) The treatment lasted three weeks already with no signs of recovery. (21) Luckily, I did recover almost totally in about six weeks. (22) I still have slight problems with my left eye—it waters quite often and feels sore occasionally—but I am so relieved that I got over it. (23) It's a terrible memory!

TEXT 2 _____

(1) I suffer from migraine attacks. (2) I've had this problem for years and asked for advice from my doctor a long time ago so I now know exactly what to do.

(3) It happens about three times a year, and I know when an attack is starting because my vision becomes blurred. (4) I usually take special medication at that point and it really helps to minimise the symptoms. (5) If I don't take the medication, I then get an absolutely splitting headache and feel really sick. (6) Sometimes I actually vomit. (7) When I take the medication, the headache is less severe and I don't feel sick but I have to lie down in a darkened room until I feel better. (8) It's not exactly a serious problem but it is very unpleasant and is often a nuisance because I never know when it's going to happen. (9) Some medical experts think that the attacks are brought on by psychological tension. (10) That may be true. (11) My attacks tend to happen when I'm very nervous or suffering from stress at work.

提示與解析

最適合 Text 1 的標題是 "An Unpleasant Experience"，而 Text 2 則適合用 "A Continuing Problem" 當作標題。從兩篇文章的第一句，就能基本得知兩篇文章中應該會用哪種時態貫穿始終。在 Text 1中，從 "... but something rather unpleasant happened to me about three years ago."（但大約三年前，有件不怎麼愉快的事情發生在我身上。），就可以清楚地看出作者是要描述一件過去的事。在 Text 2 中，從 "I suffer from migraine attacks."（我遭受頭痛之苦。）可知，作者一直到現在還是有頭痛的問題，且這個問題從過去持續到現在仍沒有好轉。因此，Text 1 大部分以過去式為主，而 Text 2 大部分以現在式為主。

　　想必你也看出來了，Text 1 說的是「一整個故事」，從發現身體的問題，一直到復原為止。我們現在就來看看這個過程中不同的階段。

　　以下這些類型的資訊都在 Text 1 中出現過。先不要看文章，而是根據資訊類型，試著判斷其出現的順序，並標出序號。前兩項已經為你做好了。

試著判斷下列事情出現的順序。

Order	Info. type	Sentence No.
＿＿	ⓐ doctor's diagnosis	＿＿
＿＿	ⓑ symptoms of the problem	＿＿
2.	ⓒ general background to the problem	＿＿
1.	ⓓ general statement of what happened and when	＿＿
＿＿	ⓔ recovery	＿＿
＿＿	ⓕ discovery of the problem	＿＿
＿＿	ⓖ visit to the doctor	＿＿
＿＿	ⓗ treatment of the problem	＿＿
＿＿	ⓘ doctor's information about problem	＿＿

提示與解析

一開始，我們應該會先讀到 "what happened and when"（什麼時候發生了什麼事），然後了解到整個問題發生的背景。然後我們會讀到症狀出現、發現問題（ⓑ 與 ⓕ），然後再讀到去看醫生（ⓖ）以及醫生說的話（ⓐ 與 ⓘ）。最後是治療（ⓗ）以及復原（ⓔ）。

也就是說，最可能的順序就是：

3. ⓑ　　4. ⓕ　　5. ⓖ　　6. ⓐ　　7. ⓘ　　8. ⓗ　　9. ⓔ

現在請回頭仔細地讀一遍 Text 1，判斷一下不同的階段用哪些句子描述。然後回到前面的練習，將句子的數字填在右欄相應的橫線上。

Unit 1　Unit 2　Unit 3　健康 Health　Unit 4

提示與解析

a (13), (14)

c (2)

e (21), (22)

g (12)

i (15), (16), (17), (18)

b (3), (4), (7), (8), (9), (10)

d (1)

f (11)

h (19), (20)

最後一句(23)則下了一個結論。

十年英語不白學，「引用他人所說的話」就這麼說

　　Text 1 的作者描述的是一件過去發生在自己身上的事，所以間接引用了醫生的話來描述自己到底出了什麼問題。這種方式叫做 "simple reported speech"。現在也請你將下面的 "reported speech" 改成 "direct speech"。第一題已經為你做好了！

❶ He told me that I had something called Bell's Palsy.

He said, "You have something called Bell's Palsy."

❷ He said that it was a fairly common problem but not very much was known about it.

❸ The doctor explained that recovery rates varied but that it would probably take about six weeks for my face to return to normal.

---

❹ He warned me that some people never recovered and others only partially recovered.

十年英語不白學，「描述生病與康復的經驗」就這麼說

現在請回想一下，你（或你身邊的人）是否有過健康方面的問題，如果有，是否得到了有效治療並迅速康復。以 Text 1 為範例，寫一段約12句的文字，描述你（或你身邊的人）曾經有過的身體健康問題與康復的經驗。寫完並修改後，將它抄到作業本上，請朋友幫你看看。

寫一段文字描述自己或他人曾經有過的身體健康問題與康復的經驗。請使用以下標題。

<u>**An Unpleasant Experience**</u>

十年英語不白學，「描述小毛病的相關資訊」就這麼說

你或許也有一些困擾你許久的小毛病，總是時不時地在你的生活中出現。比如有些人很容易感冒，有些人則有支氣管炎（bronchitis）。有些人很容易肚子不舒服，還有些人常會便秘（constipated）。現在我們就來仔細看看前面172頁的 Text 2 描述的情形。用做筆記的方式，完成以下表格。

閱讀 Text 2，完成表格。

Problem	
Symptoms	
Frequency	
Causes	
Treatment	

提示與解析

Problem: suffer from migraine attacks
Symptoms: vision becomes blurred; splitting headache; vomit
Frequency: about three times a year
Causes: psychological tension; nervous or suffer from stress at work
Treatment: take special medication

十年英語不白學，「描述病痛發作的症狀」就這麼說

現在請利用你在表格中寫下的資訊，完成以下關於頭痛發作（Migraine Attacks）的描述。有些空格須填入不只一個單字。如果你需要參考 Text 2，可以翻回去再次閱讀。

 完成以下描述。

Migraine Attacks

Many people suffer from (1) _____.　The attacks occur (2) _____.　They may be caused by (3) _____. When an attack is starting, the patient's (4) _____.　At that point, the patient should take (5) _____.　Otherwise, he / she may get a splitting (6) _____ and feel (7) _____.　The best treatment is to (8) _____ in a (9) _____ room until the problem (10) _____.

提示與解析

1. migraine attacks

2. regularly / often / frequently / about three times a year

3. psychological tension

4. vision becomes blurred

5. medication

6. headache

7. (really) sick

8. lie down

9. darkened

10. goes away / disappears

十年英語不白學，「詢問疾病的細節」就這麼說

你有沒有聽過別人描述你從來沒聽過的病症呢？我就常遇到這種狀況，這時，我會問幾個問題，更深入地了解這種病症，例如 "frequency" "symptoms" "treatment" 等。這些問題用英文怎麼問呢？請把你可能會問的問題寫在下面。

✏️ **寫下詢問關於病症的問題。**

❶ (what)

_____

❷ (frequency)

_____

❸ (symptoms)

_____

❹ (treatment)

_____

提示與解析

寫下問題以後，可以試著說說看。
❶ What is...? 或 What is it exactly?
❷ How often does it happen? 或 How often do you get it?
❸ What are the symptoms?
❹ What is the treatment? 或 How do you treat it? 或 What do you do when it happens?

十年英語不白學，「討論一種長期持續的疾病」就這麼說

你或身邊的親友是否有什麼長期的疾病呢？參考 Text 2，想想看你會如何描述病症出現的頻率、症狀、治療方式等，並練習和其他人談論這個疾病。

Part 3——
社交英語無師自通，
道地的「醫療問診」該怎麼說？

十年英語不白學，
「回答有關病症資訊」就這麼說

聽聽看王玲與鮑勃（Bob）的對話。聽第一遍時，請先專注於下述問題：

a) What's the problem?

b) How did it happen?

c) What is the treatment?

🔊 聽音檔，做筆記。 🔊 *Track 009*

_____

_____

_____

_____

_____

提示與解析

Problem: a cut finger

How it happened: She was slicing onions.

Treatment:

（這個比較難聽懂對吧？沒關係，我們在下一個練習中會更詳細地討論這點。）

十年英語不白學，「按照事情發生的先後順序描述狀況時」就這麼說

　　意外一發生，王玲和鮑勃很快就開始行動。他們做了很多事，再聽一遍對話，將以下的事情按照發生的順序排列。在鮑勃所做的事旁邊寫下 B，王玲所做的事旁邊寫下 WL。

🔊 聽音檔，標出事情發生的順序以及哪件事是誰做的。

◀ *Track 009*

No.		Who?
____	held it up	____
____	put Soothene on the cut finger	____
____	washed his / her hand	____
____	held it under the cold tap	____
____	put a plaster on	____
____	squeezed her finger	____

提示與解析

No.		Who?
3	held it up	WL
5	put Soothene on the cut finger	B
4	washed his / her hand	B
2	held it under the cold tap	WL
6	put a plaster on	B
1	squeezed her finger	WL

"Soothene" 是一種藥膏的名字。王玲問了鮑勃："What is it?"（這是什麼？）他回答："Just an antiseptic cream that soothes the pain and helps prevent infection."（只是一種抗菌藥膏，能夠止痛、預防感染。）

十年英語不白學，
「描述傷口處理的正確步驟」就這麼說

　　從鮑勃對王玲說的話中，我們可以得知如何止血、如何處理切傷的手指。完成以下相關的指示，有些空格需要填入不只一個單字。

完成以下指示。

If you have cut your finger, you should first (1) _____ to try to stop the bleeding. Then, you should (2) _____ to make sure it's clean. After that, you should (3) _____ it up. Finally, put on some (4) _____ to soothe it, and then, a (5) _____ to protect it.

提示與解析

1. squeeze it
2. hold it under the tap
3. hold
4. cream / ointment / Soothene
5. plaster

十年英語不白學，「對患者和協助者提供指示時」就這麼說

下頁的 Text 1 說明了如何止住鼻血。如果你仔細讀，就會發現其中提供了兩組指示：給負責幫助止血的人的指示和給正在流鼻血的人的指示。從下面方框中選擇合適的選項，提供指示。

請為「幫助止血的人」寫下一組指示，說明應該怎麼做，然後再寫下另一組指示，讓「幫助止血的人」可以告訴「患者」怎麼做。兩組指示我都提供了一個例子，請把其他的部分完成。

---

a. Squeeze...   *b. Sit...*   *c. Do not... (three times)*   *d. Pinch...*
e. Get...   *f. Wait...*   *g. Check...*   *h. Tell...*   *i. Soak...*

 寫下指示。

A. For the helper

B. For the patient

1. Do not panic.

1. Do not panic.

Text 1

Nose Bleeds

Nose bleeding can be rather frightening for both the patient and any witnesses! Lots of blood always looks quite shocking, doesn't it? The main thing, as in all medical matters, is not to panic. You should first encourage the patient to sit down and then tell him / her to pinch the lower part of the nose between his / her finger and thumb and wait at least ten minutes. While the patient is seated, make sure you get paper tissues or a soft cloth ready to mop up any blood. After ten minutes, you should check to see whether the blood is still flowing. If it is, the patient should squeeze his / her nose for a further ten minutes. Advise the patient not to sniff or blow his / her nose until he / she is sure that bleeding has stopped. Remember to soak any blood-stained clothes in water as quickly as possible.

提示與解析

在發生意外時，指示的語氣通常都很直接，一般用原形動詞來開頭。

The instructions for the helper:

2. Tell the patient to sit down and pinch his / her nose and wait.
3. Get paper tissues or a soft cloth ready.
4. Check to see if the blood is still flowing.
5. Soak any blood-stained clothes in water.

The instructions for the patient:

2. Sit down.
3. Pinch your nose.

4. Wait ten minutes.
5. Squeeze your nose again if the blood is still flowing.
6. Do not sniff or blow your nose until the bleeding has stopped.

　　想想看，日常生活中是否有什麼與意外或健康問題相關的情況，使你必須幫人提供正確的指示呢？如果要用英文發出這些指令，你會怎麼說呢？如果你想不出來有什麼情況需要發出指令的，可以揣摩一下以下情境：

cramp in the leg（腿抽筋）
pins and needles in the foot（腳麻）
something in the eye（東西跑進眼睛）
hiccups（打嗝）

別忘了，在下指令時，要用原形動詞。

 練習下指令。

Part 4——
社交英語無師自通，
道地的「各式藥品」該怎麼說？

十年英語不白學，
「藥品上的標籤說明」就這麼說

　　現在藥品種類越來越多了，為了搞清楚到底每種藥的用途是什麼，我們應該學會看藥盒、藥罐、藥包上都寫了什麼。下面的 Text 1 到 Text 5 是一些藥品的標籤，請看看這些標籤，完成下面的表格。在第二欄中請寫下這種藥品的形式，如：powder（粉末），liquid（液體），tablets（藥片），pills（藥丸），cream（膏狀）等。在第三欄中，寫下這種藥品的用途。第一種已經為你寫好了。

閱讀 Texts 1～5, 完成表格。

Name	Form	Functions
Parapain	*tablets*	*for headaches, rheumatic pains, neuralgia, colds, influenza*
Inban		
Vitese		
Hit		
Soothene		

Text 1

PARAPAIN (25 TABLETS BP.)

For headaches, rheumatic pains, neuralgia and relief of symptoms of colds and influenza.

DOSE UNLESS OTHERWISE DIRECTED BY A DOCTOR

Adults and children over 12 years, swallow one to two tablets with water. Dose should not be repeated more frequently than 4-hour intervals and not more than 4 times in any 24-hour period.

DO NOT EXCEED THE STATED DOSE. AN OVERDOSE IS DANGEROUS. MEDICAL ATTENTION SHOULD BE SOUGHT IMMEDIATELY.

Text 2

INBAN Liquid Insect Repellent

Protects against insect bites for 6-8 hours

Provide 6-8 hours protection against gnats, mosquitoes, midges and other biting insects. Apply carefully to all unprotected parts of the body. Keep out of reach of children. Avoid contact with eyes, nose and mouth, also with plastic, nylon and varnished surfaces.

Text 3

VITESE Cold Relief Powder

Fast relief from colds and flu with extra vitamin C

How to take this medicine:

√ Check that each powder sachet is intact before use. Adults and children over 12 years: empty the contents of 1 sachet into a beaker or tumbler, fill with freshly boiled water and stir until fully dissolved. Sweeten to taste if desired. Take at bedtime and repeat every 4 hours if necessary.

For children 3 to 12 years: we recommend Viteeze Cold Relief for Children.

x Do not take more than 4 doses in 24 hours. Do not exceed the stated dose. Children under 12 should not be given this medicine without medical advice.

Contains Paracetamol

Do not take other medicines containing Paracetamol while using this product.

! If symptoms do not go away, talk to your doctor. Keep all medicines out of the reach of children.

Text 4

HIT Liquid Antiseptic   Dual-action   (soothes pain + fights infection)
For: sore throats, mouth ulcers, cuts and grazes, bites and stings, spots

Sore throats
Simply gargle twice a day HIT diluted with five parts water
Mouth ulcers
To ease the discomfort of common mouth ulcers, dab undiluted three times
a day. Should symptoms persist for more than fourteen days, consult your
doctor or dentist.
Cuts, grazes, bites and stings
Dilute with an equal quantity of water and apply freely. In emergencies
may be used undiluted.
Boils, spots and pimples
Dab undiluted every four hours.
Seek medical assistance if symptoms persist for more than a few days.

KEEP OUT OF CHILDREN'S REACH.

Text 5

Soothene Antiseptic Cream

Soothene helps natural healing   **FOR EXTERNAL USE ONLY**
Indications: prevents infection, and aids the natural healing
For: cuts, grazes, minor burns and scalds, blisters, sunburn,
insect bites and stings
Directions: with clean hands, gently smear the cream over
the affected area
If symptoms persist, stop using and consult your doctor.

KEEP OUT OF EYES.

2. Inban is a liquid insect repellent. It protects against gnats, mosquitoes, midges and other biting insects.

3. Vitese is a powder. It is for colds and flu.

4. Hit is a liquid antiseptic. It is for sore throats, mouth ulcers, cuts and grazes, bites and stings and spots.

5. Soothene is a cream. It is for cuts, grazes, minor burns and scalds, blisters, sunburn, insect bites and stings.

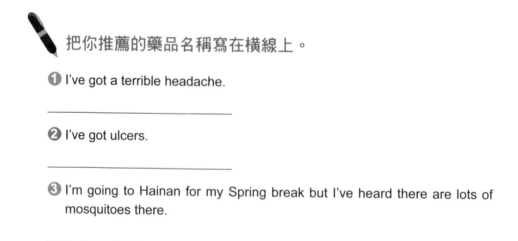

十年英語不白學，「推薦適合的藥品」就這麼說

　　現在你已經知道上述藥品的用途了，請看看以下的情境。想像你的朋友在向你描述他們的症狀或需求，需要你幫忙推薦合適的藥品給他們。

把你推薦的藥品名稱寫在橫線上。

❶ I've got a terrible headache.

――――――――――――――――

❷ I've got ulcers.

――――――――――――――――

❸ I'm going to Hainan for my Spring break but I've heard there are lots of mosquitoes there.

――――――――――――――――

④ My son has a sore graze on his knee. I don't know what to use.

_____

⑤ I have awful blisters on my heels from that long walk we had yesterday.

_____

**十年英語不白學，
「口頭描述你所推薦的藥品時」就這麼說**

　　現在想像一下，如果要和別人討論這些藥品，可以怎麼說呢？可以參考以下的對話。

B: <u>What's wrong with you?</u>
A: Oh, I've got a bad cold. I really feel awful.
B: <u>Have you tried Vitese?</u>　　OR　　<u>Why don't you try Vitese?</u>
A: What did you say it was called?
B: <u>Vitese... V-I-T-E-S-E.</u>
A: What is it exactly?
B: <u>Well, it is a powder that you mix with hot water. It has a lot of vitamin C in it, and contains paracetemol as well.</u>
A: Where can I buy it?
B: <u>In any chemist's.</u>

十年英語不白學，「藥品的中文名稱」就這麼說

　　藥品的種類很多，像是前面提到的Parapain是藥片（tablet），Vitese 是粉末狀（powder），Hit 與 Inban是液體（liquid），Soothene 則是膏狀（cream）。下面的方框中還有一些其他的例子，請將方框中的英文與下方的中文匹配。

a. ointment	b. capsule	c. syrup	d. plaster
e. liquid antiseptic	f. drops	g. pills	h. lotion

❶ 膏藥　　　　　　❷ 膠囊
❸ 滴劑　　　　　　❹ 藥膏
❺ 糖漿　　　　　　❻ 洗劑
❼ 藥片　　　　　　❽ 殺菌液、消毒液

提示與解析

❶ d　　❷ b　　❸ f　　❹ a　　❺ c　　❻ h　　❼ g　　❽ e

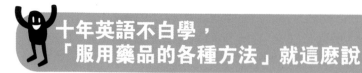

十年英語不白學，「服用藥品的各種方法」就這麼說

 從以下方框中選出適當的動詞（片語），完成下面的句子。每個動詞（片語）只會使用一次。

dab	take	drink	apply
gargle	put on	swallow	use

① I hear you've got a stiff neck. You can _____ this ointment once every day.

② You're coughing so seriously. Why not try this cough syrup? _____ it three times a day.

③ These pills are to keep the fever down. _____ two with boiled water when your temperature goes up.

④ This capsule is very effective for colds and flu. _____ one every four hours, and I'm sure you will feel much better in a couple of days.

⑤ I'm afraid your finger has got infected. This lotion can keep the swelling down. _____ it on the swollen part every three hours.

⑥ I think this liquid antiseptic will relieve your sore throat. _____ with it when you feel uncomfortable in your throat.

⑦ These eye drops may soothe your sore eye. _____ a few drops when you go to bed every night.

⑧ I see you have a nasty cut on your thumb. Why not _____ a plaster?

提示與解析

答案：
① apply
② Drink
③ Swallow / Take
④ Swallow / Take
⑤ Dab
⑥ Gargle
⑦ Use
⑧ put on

Part 5——
社交英語無師自通，
道地的「和醫生交談」該怎麼說？

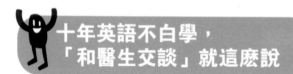
十年英語不白學，
「和醫生交談」就這麼說

　　請聽一段與健康有關的對話。聽音檔前，先看看以下的問題，了解對話的重點。然後聽音檔，選擇正確的答案。有些問題不只一個答案。

🔊 聽音檔，選擇正確的答案。　◀ *Track 010*

❶ When and where does this conversation take place?
　a. In the afternoon, at home.
　b. In the morning, in a doctor's surgery.
　c. In the evening, at a party.
　d. In the morning, at home.
　e. In the evening, in a doctor's surgery.
　f. In the afternoon, at a party.

❷ What is the relationship between the two speakers? How can you tell?
　a. They are husband and wife. We know because the woman is complaining about her illness in detail.
　b. They are neighbours. They are discussing the woman's health problem and the man is rather helpful.
　c. They are doctor and patient. We can tell from the questions asked or comments made by the man who is clearly a doctor.
　d. They are host and guest at a party. The man, the host, is very concerned about the woman's health and they discuss the woman's illness in detail.

❸ What health problem does the woman describe to the man?
  a. The woman tells the man that she has got an upset stomach and she feels extremely weak.
  b. The woman tells the man that she has got a terrible headache and can't sleep well.
  c. The woman tells the man that she has got constipation and she keeps running to the bathroom.
  d. The woman tells the man that she has got a bad cold and she keeps feeling hot and cold.

❹ What symptoms does the woman have?
  a. She has been vomiting.
  b. She keeps feeling sick.
  c. She has got diarrhoea and keeps running to the bathroom.
  d. She has a poor appetite and doesn't feel like eating.
  e. She feels tired all the time and is sleeping more than usual.
  f. She feels hot and cold.

❺ What conclusion does the man draw?
  a. The woman is suffering from indigestion.
  b. The woman has got a high fever.
  c. The woman has a touch of food poisoning.
  d. The woman has a hangover.

❻ Has the woman ever had this problem before?
  a. Never.
  b. Once or twice every year.
  c. Several times in the last few years.
  d. Once or twice when she was quite young.

7 What does the man prescribe for the woman's illness?

    a. Some syrup which the woman should drink three times a day.

    b. Some pills that the woman should take with warm water three times a day.

    c. Some liquid antiseptic that the woman should gargle with whenever she feels uncomfortable.

    d. A plaster that the woman should put on her stomach once a day.

8 What advice does the man give to the woman?

    a. Go home and take a day off.

    b. Go back to work and don't worry about the illness.

    c. Drink lots of water.

    d. Drink as little water as possible.

    e. Stay away from fruit juice, tea and coffee.

    f. Drink fruit juice, tea and coffee as much as possible.

    g. Eat simple, dry food.

    h. Eat rich, fat food.

    i. Eat some plain yoghurt.

    j. Don't eat any kind of yoghurt because it is bad for stomach.

提示與解析

❶ b	❷ c	❸ a	❹ b, c, d, e, f
❺ c	❻ d	❼ b	❽ a, c, e, g, i

透過這些問題和答案，我們已經能大概猜到整段對話的大意了。病人的名字是泰特（Tate），她正在和醫生談論她腸胃不適的問題。

十年英語不白學，「詢問病人症狀時」就這麼說

　　醫生幫病人看病時，通常會先問一個比較概括的問題，然後再逐步深入詢問病人的症狀，以便做出判斷。聽音檔，完成以下句子。

🔊 聽音檔，並完成以下句子。　◀ *Track 010*

❶ _____ seems to be the _____?

❷ _____ _____ _____ vomiting?

❸ _____ _____ _____ diarrhoea?

❹ When did this _____?

❺ Did you eat anything _____?

❻ _____ _____ appetite now?

❼ And what about _____?

❽ Have you noticed _____ _____ _____?

提示與解析

你會發現，醫生問的第一個問題非常概括。

❶ <u>What</u> seems to be the <u>matter</u>?
❷ <u>Have</u> <u>you</u> <u>been</u> vomiting?
❸ <u>Have</u> <u>you</u> <u>got</u> diarrhoea?
❹ When did this <u>start</u>?
❺ Did you eat anything <u>unusual</u>?
❻ <u>How's</u> <u>your</u> appetite now?
❼ And what about <u>sleep</u>?
❽ Have you noticed <u>any</u> <u>other</u> <u>symptoms</u>?

醫生發現病人腸胃不舒服後，就開始問一些比較精確的問題，尤其是一些相關的症狀，如嘔吐、拉肚子等，他可以透過這些症狀幫助病人找出病因。

十年英語不白學，
「向醫生描述身體狀況時」就這麼說

聽音檔，記錄下泰特的症狀，並將它們寫在下方空白處。我已經為你寫好第一個了！

🔊 聽音檔並記錄泰特的症狀。 ◀ *Track 010*

❶ *I've got an upset stomach.*

❷ I feel _____.

❸ I keep feeling _____.

❹ I keep running _____.

❺ I just don't feel _____.

❻ I feel _____.

❼ I keep feeling _____.

提示與解析

2 I feel <u>extremely weak</u>.

3 I keep feeling <u>sick</u>.

4 I keep running <u>to the bathroom</u>.

5 I just don't feel <u>like eating</u>.

6 I feel <u>tired all the time</u>.

7 I keep feeling <u>hot and cold</u>.

社交英語無師自通，你一定還想知道更多！

泰特在描述症狀時，用了如下三種句型：

• I've got (an upset stomach).

• I keep (feeling sick; running to the bathroom; feeling hot and cold).

• I feel (tired; extremely weak).

請注意，雖然 "I've" 是 "I have" 的縮寫，但我們通常會說 "I've got"，很少會有人在描述疾病時說 "I have got"。另外，美式英文不太常用 "I've got"，而會直接說：I have a headache.

"I've got an upset stomach." 也可以說成 "My stomach is upset." 現在練習把下面的句子改寫成 "My... is / are..." 的形式。第一句已經為你寫好了！

 改寫以下句子。

1 I've got a hum in my ears.

My ears are humming.

❷ I've got a stuffed-up nose.

_____

❸ I've got a sore throat.

_____

❹ I've got a toothache.

_____

❺ I've got swollen glands.

_____

❻ I've got an infected finger.

_____

❼ I've got a twisted ankle.

_____

❽ I've got high blood pressure.

_____

提示與解析

❷ My nose is stuffed up.　　❸ My throat is sore.
❹ My tooth is aching.　　❺ My glands are swollen.
❻ My finger is infected.　　❼ My ankle is twisted.
❽ My blood pressure is high.

十年英語不白學，「向病人說明診斷時」就這麼說

在詢問了病人的症狀後，醫生通常就可以做出診斷，告訴病人可能的病因。醫生可能會說：

It sounds as if...
It sounds like...
It looks as if...
It looks like...

剛才音檔中的對話，醫生就對泰特說：It sounds as if you have a touch of food poisoning.

請注意 "sound like" 和 "look like" 後面接的是名詞或名詞片語。而 "sounds as if" 與 "looks as if" 後面則是接一整個句子。
請試著改寫下面的句子。

 改寫以下句子。

❶ It sounds like bronchitis. (It sounds as if...)
It sounds as if you have bronchitis.

❷ It looks like measles. (It looks as if...)
_____.

❸ It sounds as if you have a heart problem. (It sounds like...)
_____.

❹ It looks as if you have got scarlet fever. (It looks like...)
_____.

❺ It sounds like low blood pressure. (It sounds as if...)

_____.

❻ It looks as if you have an allergic reaction. (It looks like...)

_____.

❼ It sounds like rheumatism. (It sounds as if...)

_____.

❽ It looks as if you have an inflammation of the skin. (It looks like...)

_____.

提示與解析

❷ It looks as if you have measles.
❸ It sounds like a heart problem.
❹ It looks like scarlet fever.
❺ It sounds as if you have low blood pressure.
❻ It looks like an allergic reaction.
❼ It sounds as if you have rheumatism.
❽ It looks like an inflammation of the skin.

這一題中，想必有許多單字你會覺得陌生。沒關係！這些單字很多都是醫學術
語，你不需要掌握，只要能夠用簡單的英文描述症狀就可以了。

最後，請再復習一遍這個單元的內容，希望以後有人與你聊到疾病、症狀相關的話題時，你能完整且正確地表達自己的意思。

學完這一單元，你就可以：

☐ 詢問關於健康的問題。

☐ 描述自己的症狀。

☐ 描述各種病症。

☐ 提供關於治療的建議。

第三單元總復習

十年英語不白學，「描述和癌症奮戰的故事」就這麼說

琳達（Linda）在和她的同事湯姆（Tom）討論關於她爸爸得癌症的事情。

🔊 聽音檔，試著回答以下問題。 ◀ *Track 011*

❶ What sort of cancer does Linda's father have?

❷ What does Linda have to do to look after him?

❸ What does she suggest Tom should do to help?

❹ Does her sister visit her father very often?

❺ What are the doctor's predictions of her father's progress?

❻ What does Tom suggest Linda should do?

❼ What stops her doing it?

❽ What does she agree to do in the end?

① Cancer of the stomach.

② Cook, liquidise all his food, change his bed sheets and drive him to the hospital for treatment every week.

③ Come and visit him and tell him about his holiday in Kenya.

④ Not much as she travels a lot, but she visits her father when she can and cheers him up, and she chooses good video films for him to watch.

⑤ Not much chance of a cure. He may live for another year if the condition stays the same, or less if it worsens.

⑥ Hire a full-time nurse to help her care for her father.

⑦ It would make her feel guilty that she's not doing her duty herself.

⑧ She agrees to start looking for a nurse the next day.

MP3音檔內容完整看

　　若是聽完音檔還是沒把握，建議可搭配本部份學習，不熟的語彙要查辭典並作筆記，方能加深英文記憶。

（請配合153、155、157、158、166頁及音檔使用）

Part 1: Track 008

Terry:	Hi, Du Wei. What's wrong with you? You don't look too good.
Du Wei:	Oh, I've got a really bad cold. My eyes are sore; I feel all stuffed up and thick-headed.
Terry:	Oh, I'm sorry to hear that. Your nose looks sore too.
Du Wei:	Yes, I know... I feel awful. I really do. I can't think straight.
Terry:	So why did you come to work? You should be at home, in bed.
Du Wei:	Perhaps... but I have to finish an assignment by Friday so I need to spend some time in the library.
Terry:	But you're sick, you poor thing. Why don't you go home? You're so weak. I'm sure you're not in a fit state to do any work.
Du Wei:	Mm... I must admit. I don't feel like doing anything except sleeping, perhaps!
Terry:	So it would be much better if you went home and went to bed... and tried to get well. Are you taking anything?
Du Wei:	Well, I'm not taking any medicine but I'm drinking lots and taking vitamin C.
Terry:	But that's not enough. Vitamin C helps prevent colds but I don't think it cures them. Have you tried Vitese? I took it a while ago when I had an awful cold and I really think it helped.
Du Wei:	What did you say it was called?
Terry:	Vitese... V-I-T-E-S-E... you can buy it in any chemist's.
Du Wei:	What is it exactly?
Terry:	Well it's a powder. You mix it with hot water and drink it. It has a lot of vitamin C in it but contains aspirin or paracetamol as well, I think. I'd

Unit 1 Unit 2 Unit 3 健康 Health Unit 4

| 207

really recommend it. It made me feel better after just a couple of doses.

Du Wei: OK then, I'll go and get some after I've been to the library.

Terry: Don't be a martyr! Don't go to the library. That's an order! Come on, I'll walk to the chemist's with you now.

Du Wei: All right. You win. I'm too weak to argue.

Terry: Come on then. Let's go. You really should take care of yourself, you know...

Du Wei: OK, OK... don't overdo the tender loving care. You sound like an old woman!

Terry: Thanks a lot! I'm only trying to help. But I know what you mean. I don't like people making a fuss when I'm ill either...

Part 3: Track 009 （請配合182、183頁及音檔使用）

Wang Ling: Ah... ow... Bob! Help! I've cut my finger.

Bob: Oh dear... it looks quite bad. Here... squeeze your finger with the other hand and then run it under the cold tap to wash all the blood away and make sure it's clean. Whatever were you doing?

Wang Ling: Just slicing some onions with that new knife. It's really sharp, huh? Umm... it hurts.

Bob: I bet it does. It looks quite deep... but it's OK. You won't die. Just keep holding it under the tap and I'll get some Soothene and a plaster.

Wang Ling: Soothene? What's that?

Bob: Just an antiseptic cream that soothes the pain and helps prevent infection. It's great. My mum never moves without it. The smell reminds me of every little injury I had when I was a child. Is it still bleeding?

Wang Ling: No, not much... but it's really throbbing.

Bob: Yes, that's normal... but hold it up... up. That will help stop the

	bleeding. And, I suppose I should wash my hands if I'm going to touch it. Just a moment...
Wang Ling:	You're very professional... Do you like playing at being a doctor?
Bob:	Oh, Wang Ling! I'm only doing what's necessary. And I did do a first aid course a few years ago... so I learnt all about minor injuries, etc.
Wang Ling:	Well, that's good news for me, I suppose.
Bob:	Yes, I guess it is! Here, let me look at it... ummm... it looks fine. I'll just put some Soothene on.
Wang Ling:	Let me see the tube... and make sure you're following the instructions. Now, what does it say...? "With clean hands"... yes, good... you washed your hands... "Smear the affected area"... Yes, you've done that. "If symptoms persist, consult your doctor". Well, I have my very own doctor, don't I? Doctor Bob!
Bob:	Well, you certainly seem OK already. You definitely don't need a doctor. Do you think we should put a sticking plaster on it?
Wang Ling:	Yes, I think so. It is still bleeding a bit.
Bob:	OK... give me your finger... there, how's that?
Wang Ling:	That's great... but I'm afraid you'll have to finish making lunch!

Part 5: Track 010   （請配合196、199、200頁及音檔使用）

Doctor:	Good morning, Mrs. Tate. Have a seat.
Mrs. Tate:	Thank you.
Doctor:	So, what seems to be the matter?
Mrs. Tate:	Well, I've got an upset stomach and I feel extremely weak.
Doctor:	An upset stomach? Have you been vomiting?
Mrs. Tate:	No, but I keep feeling sick.
Doctor:	And have you got diarrhoea?

Mrs. Tate: Yes, I have. I keep running to the bathroom.

Doctor: I see. And when did this start?

Mrs. Tate: Three days ago. I thought it would go away quickly but I can't seem to get rid of it.

Doctor: Did you eat anything unusual?

Mrs. Tate: No, not that I can think of. I had eaten in a good restaurant the night before it started.

Doctor: Ummm... And how's your appetite now?

Mrs. Tate: Well, I just don't feel like eating. And every time I do eat something, I have to run to the bathroom almost immediately.

Doctor: And what about sleep? Are you sleeping normally?

Mrs. Tate: Well, I feel tired all the time so I'm sleeping more than usual. I feel so weak, you see.

Doctor: Have you noticed any other symptoms?

Mrs. Tate: I keep feeling hot and cold.

Doctor: It sounds as if you have a touch of food poisoning. Let me take your temperature. Here, just pop this under your tongue.

(*Pause*)

Doctor: Yes, I'm fairly certain that you've got food poisoning. Lots of people get food poisoning at some point in their lives. Now, let me take your temperature... Ummm... it's a bit higher than normal but not too bad. Yes, I should say you've got food poisoning. Have you ever had this problem before?

Mrs. Tate: I think I had it once or twice when I was a child.

Doctor: Well, I'm prescribing some medication—some pills. You should take two three times a day for the next three days, with water, warm water. They should do the trick. You should be better by the weekend.

Mrs. Tate: Do you think I am well enough to go to work?

Doctor: That's really up to you. I should go home now, if I were you, and then see how you feel in the morning.

Mrs. Tate: What about food? Should I eat normally?

Doctor: Well, you should give your stomach a bit of time to recover. Make sure you drink lots of water. Stay away from fruit juices, tea and coffee. Eat simple, dry food—you know, bread, plain rice, biscuits, that sort of thing. Plain yoghurt often helps stomach problems. But don't worry. You'll soon be well. Here's your prescription. Just take to the chemist's.

Mrs. Tate: Thank you. Thank you very much.

Doctor: And, don't hesitate to come back to see me if, by any chance, you haven't recovered by the weekend.

Mrs. Tate: I'll do that. Thank you. Goodbye.

Doctor: Bye.

Fighting Cancer

Tom: Hi Linda! Say, you're looking a bit tired. Are you all right?

Linda: Oh, hi Tom. Yes, I'm fine.

Tom: Are you sure? You don't look fine.

Linda: Oh, it's my father. His cancer is getting worse and I have to spend a lot of time looking after him.

Tom: Oh dear. I'm sorry to hear that. Is there anything I can do to help?

Linda: Well, you could come and see him occasionally. He really needs cheering up, and he forgets his pain a little when he has someone to talk to. I know, he'd love to hear about your recent holiday in Kenya.

Tom: OK, I'll bring him my photos. I have some great ones of wild animals in the safari park. His eyesight is still OK, isn't it?

Linda: Oh, yes. It's his stomach that's the problem. The pain is terrible and he can only eat liquids. So, I have to liquidise all his food—you know a lot of good nutritious soups and things.

Tom: Oh gosh. It really is a lot of work for you. Can't the National Health Service provide a nurse to help you?

Linda: Well, they give us a Health Visitor who comes once a week and checks on him and makes him feel a little more comfortable. But it's the daily things that I need help with, like cooking and changing his bed sheets, and trying to bathe him.

Tom: What about your sister? Can't she help?

Linda: Not much. Her work keeps her very busy—you know she's a sales representative, so she has to travel a lot. She does come and see him when she can though, and does her best to cheer him up. She's very good at choosing video films for him, so he watches those while I'm out at work. That keeps him occupied a little. Of course, he sleeps a lot too.

Tom: Does he still have to go to the hospital regularly?

Linda: Yes, I drive him there once a week. They are still giving him treatment, though they say there's little they can do now to cure him.

Tom: Yes, cancer of the stomach is a terrible thing. How long do they think he has left?

Linda: They say maybe a year, if it continues like this. If it gets worse, he'll go much quicker.

Tom: Well, I really think you need to hire a full-time nurse to help you, Linda. You can't possibly manage a full-time job and look after your father. You need your strength too, you know! You must look after your own health.

Linda: Yes, Tom, I suppose you're right. I should stop trying to be a hero by doing it all myself. I suppose, I'd feel really guilty about hiring someone else to look after him, as I feel it's my duty.

Tom: Oh, Linda, I'm sure your father would understand. He doesn't want to see you looking tired all the time. Plus the nurse would keep him company while you're out at work.

Linda: Yes, you're right, Tom. I'll start looking for someone tomorrow. Now when are you going to come and see him?

Tom: Oh, I'll come round this evening.

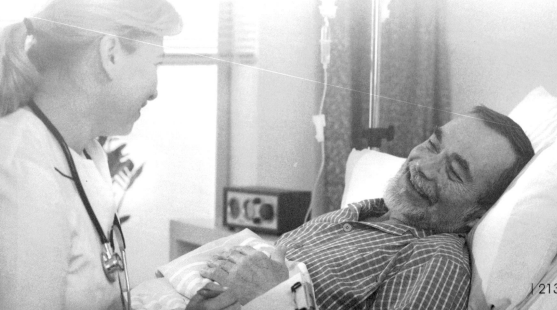

Unit 1 | Unit 2 | Unit 3 健康 Health | Unit 4

NOTE

NOTE

Unit 4 人生百態
People

Unit 4 人生百態

People

　　這個單元談論的是社會中不同群體之間的關係。人們透過交往能帶給彼此快樂，但同時也會產生一些問題。在這個單元中，我們會討論一些這樣的問題，大家一起來想想這些問題該如何溝通和解決。

十年英語不白學，「人生的七個階段」你怎麼說？

　　人的生命通常會經歷七個階段：嬰兒時期（babyhood）、剛學步的幼童時期（the toddler stage）、童年（childhood）、十幾歲的青少年時期（the teenage years）、青年時期（young adulthood period）、中年時期（middle age）、老年時期（old age）。在這裡，"toddler" 和 "toddle" 這個動詞相關，"toddle" 的意思是剛學步的幼童用碎步、不穩的方式走路。你想過人的生命的各個階段有多長嗎？每個階段又是從何時開始、在何時結束呢？請把你的想法寫在下面的表格中。

 判斷人生各階段開始與結束的時間。

Stage	From	Till
babyhood	*birth*	
the toddler stage		
childhood		

the teenage years		
young adulthood period		
middle age		
old age		*death*

提示與解析

首先要告訴大家：人生各階段之間的分界線並不明顯，每個人或每種文化的界定可能都不同。也就是說，沒有什麼標準答案，只要你的答案範圍符合常識即可。

一般而言，"babyhood" 大約是從出生開始到18個月左右，這時一般的孩子應該可以開始慢慢學步了。"toddler" 階段大概從19個月開始到2~3歲左右，這時一般的孩子慢慢可以穩步行走了。"childhood" 大約從2~3歲到12歲左右。"teenage years" 指的就是數字裡面出現 "teen" 的歲數（thirteen，fourteen 等），所以從13歲到19歲都算是 "teenage years"。
總體而言，前面四個階段比較容易判斷，因為每個階段基本都有明確的特徵指示。但剩下的三個階段就比較難說了，人們對 "middle age" 和 "old age" 何時開始常有不同的看法。在西方社會中，人們漸漸開始避免使用 "old age" "old people" "an old woman" 等說法，因為用 "old" 這個字給人感覺似乎比較負面。所以現在人們稱60歲或65歲以上的人為 "senior citizens"，或用比較級稱他們為 "an older man" 或 "an older woman"。不過在中文裡，「老」這個字的含義和 "old" 並不太相同，「老」可以用來尊稱別人。

Part 1——
社交英語無師自通，
道地的「人與人之間的肢體接觸」該怎麼說？

十年英語不白學，
「描述袋鼠」就這麼說

　　雖然這個單元講的是人，但我們先來討論一下袋鼠（kangaroos）。感覺有點奇怪嗎？到下一個練習你就知道為什麼了。你知道哪些關於袋鼠的知識？請寫在下面的空白處。例如：它們是什麼樣的動物？是鳥類（birds）還是哺乳類（mammals）呢？它們住在哪裡？它們是怎樣活動的？袋鼠媽媽如何帶著寶寶到處走動？

　　寫下你對袋鼠的了解。

kangaroos: _____

_____

提示與解析

Kangaroos are mammals.（袋鼠是哺乳類。）
They live in Australia.（牠們住在澳洲。）
They jump along on large back legs.（牠們用大大的後腿跳著移動。）
Females carry their young in a sort of pocket on their stomachs.（母袋鼠會把寶寶裝在肚子上的袋裡。）

你覺得人類是不是可以跟袋鼠學學呢？請讀一讀下頁的 Text 1，看看醫學專家對此的看法。

十年英語不白學，「有關家庭生活的文章標題」就這麼說

　　以下的文章選取自一本雜誌 *Family World* 《家庭世界》。你可以從雜誌的名字看出這本雜誌中的文章一定和家庭生活有關。先快速瀏覽一遍這篇文章，選出最合適的標題。

閱讀短文 Text 1，選出最合適的標題。

ⓐ Let's Live with Kangaroos
ⓑ The Mother and Her Premature Infant
ⓒ Let's Learn from Kangaroos
ⓓ Kangaroos Take Care of Human Babies

Text 1

　　When it comes to care of babies who are born prematurely, we can learn a thing or two from kangaroos. Babies who are born earlier than the expected date in one of London's biggest hospitals are no longer isolated in incubators, far away from their mothers for the earlier weeks of their lives. The hospital encourages parents (both Mums and Dads) to cuddle their babies to their chest for a few hours each day. In other words, the parents take the place of the incubator and, at the same time, establish a physical bond with the baby.

　　It's an idea that comes straight from the animal world, from kangaroos who nurture their young in pouches on their chest.

　　"Parents want to be more involved in caring for their babies," says Nancy Easton, coordinator of the hospital baby care programme. While kangaroo care is not suitable for all premature babies (some are too fragile), studies show that it helps many infants thrive. Everyone agrees it makes both babies and parents much happier.

以下方框中的單字都在 Text 1 中出現過。下面提供了一些定義，請將單字與定義配對。如果不知道某些單字的意思，可以再讀一遍 Text 1，試著根據上下文推斷詞義。請把相應的單字寫在橫線上。

 將單字與定義配對。

cuddle	incubator	bond	nurture
pouch	fragile	thrive	premature

❶ _premature_ earlier than expected

❷ _____ to give care and food

❸ _____ weak; not in good health

❹ _____ a machine for keeping alive babies that are too small to live and breathe in ordinary air

❺ _____ to develop well and be healthy

❻ _____ relationship; a feeling that unites two or more people or groups

❼ _____ to hold somebody lovingly and closely in the arms

❽ _____ a kind of pocket of skin in the lower half of the body in which certain animals carry their young

提示與解析

2 nurture　**3** fragile　**4** incubator　**5** thrive
6 bond　**7** cuddle　**8** pouch

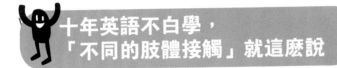

十年英語不白學，「不同的肢體接觸」就這麼說

　　Text 1中強調父母和孩子之間肢體接觸的重要性。文中說，父母應該要多摟抱孩子，這樣不但孩子開心，父母心情也會比較愉悅。不同社會的人，對於肢體接觸也有不同的看法，有些人不太介意，有些人則不太喜歡。根據自己的生活經驗，或者讀過的書、看過的電影，想一想在不同的社會中，有哪些肢體接觸的方式可以用來打招呼呢？這裡談的「肢體接觸」是指在公共場合適宜的接觸，請把你的想法寫在以下空白處。

　　寫下打招呼用的不同的肢體接觸方式。

_____

_____

_____

_____

_____

_____

_____

shaking hands, hugging, kissing, patting, stroking, etc.

握手（shaking hands）是一種很常見的打招呼方式，不過有些場合握手又顯得太正式了。但在英國，如果一個父親和他許久不見的兒子握手，是很正常的。母親則可能會擁抱（hug）或親吻（kiss）她的孩子。在法國、義大利等歐洲城市，親朋好友在見面時親吻對方臉頰是很正常的事，同時也可能擁抱或握手，視雙方有多親近而定。有些人也會邊握手邊拍對方的背（pat each other），甚至輕撫（stroke）對方。近年來在英美各地，擁抱與親吻在年輕人之間已經越來越常見了。許多人覺得這樣的肢體接觸能幫助大家放鬆下來。

請注意，雖然 "hugging"（擁抱）和 "cuddling"（摟抱）類似，但 "hugging" 通常比較短暫，而 "cuddling" 則持續比較久。你可能也見過 "bear hug" 這個說法，直譯就是「熊抱」，也就是力量很大的擁抱！

Part 2—
社交英語無師自通，
道地的「關於當爸媽的事情」該怎麼說？

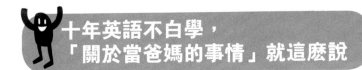

**十年英語不白學，
「關於當爸媽的事情」就這麼說**

　　Part 1 中，我們學到親子之間肢體接觸的重要性。親子之間有很多相處的方式，如果你自己身為父母，一定很清楚當個好爸爸、好媽媽有多複雜吧！接下來我們將讀到 Text 2，其中作者描述了對「父母」這個角色的個人看法。快速讀一下這篇文章，選出最恰當的選項。你讀到哪些文字，才決定要選擇這個選項呢？將這些文字寫在題目下方的空白處。

　選出最能代表此文章作者想法的選項，並寫出讓你選擇此選項的文字。

He / She thinks parenthood is _____.

ⓐ wonderful

ⓑ difficult and stressful

ⓒ terrible

ⓓ enjoyable but expensive

The words which led me to my decision are:

_____

Text 2

Happily ever after?

We all know what happened to Cinderella. She fell in love with Prince Charming, married him and they lived happily ever after. Or did they?

As children, we're brought up on romantic fairy tales that never seem to mention what happened when the happy couple became parents. As adults we're faced with glossy magazines and TV images of the joys of parenthood. So it's not surprising that many parents are shocked and disappointed when they discover that real life isn't always like that. Parenthood is often characterised by worry, anxiety and a feeling of failure. This reality can even make some parents feel that there's something wrong with them.

Being a parent is perhaps the most difficult and demanding job that you can do. There are many things that can make it even more stressful—like unemployment, lack of money, cramped living conditions, difficulties at work, illness, not understanding your children's behaviour, or your own relationship problems.

When parents are under a lot of stress, their children can suffer too. Children don't understand adult problems or emotions. If their parents are often cross or bad-tempered, children will begin to worry that they are somehow to blame. They can't solve the problems so it is every parent's responsibility to learn to deal with stress.

提示與解析

你會發現，這篇文章的標題最後用的是問號。這是為什麼呢？
你可以一邊思考這個問題，一邊看文章中的用詞。你有沒有發現 "shocked"（驚訝的），"disappointed"（失望的），"stressful"（壓力大的），"difficulties"（各種困難），"suffer"（受苦），"cross"（不高興的），"bad-tempered"（壞脾氣的），"worry"（煩惱），"blame"（責怪）這些單字呢？你覺得它們的意思是什麼？這位作者覺得，當父母既困難壓力又大，所以，他才會在標題中用一個問號，表示他對 "happily ever after"（永遠幸福快樂）這件事存疑，也就是說「結婚生子就會幸福快樂嗎？這很難說！」因而作者的觀點是 ⓑ。你覺得呢？你同意作者的觀點嗎？

再看一遍文章，回答下面的問題。

閱讀並回答問題。

❶ Which aspects of childhood life encourage us to believe that parenthood is a happy experience?

_____

❷ Which aspects of adulthood life encourage us to believe that parenthood is a happy experience?

_____

❸ Why does the reality of parenthood make some people feel that there is something wrong with them?

_____

❹ Why should parents learn to deal with stress?

_____

❺ Text 2 is only the first part of an article. We have not included the second part. Can you guess what topic the second part would cover?

_____

提示與解析

❶ Romantic fairy tales.

❷ Glossy magazines and TV images of the joys of parenthood.

❸ Because reality is very different from the happy images that have been given.

❹ Because children can suffer too when parents are under a lot of stress. They would worry that they are somehow to blame.

❺ Ways of dealing with stress for parents.

十年英語不白學，「關於對當爸媽的看法」就這麼說

　　從 Text 2 以及自己的經驗中，相信你已經知道做父母不是那麼容易。但不同的人對做父母這件事情也有很多不同的看法。西方國家的研究調查指出，90%的成人都會當父母，而其中又有三分之一的人會有兩個或兩個以上孩子。這和華人的情形不完全一樣，但相信大部分的人都還是至少會有一個孩子。既然做父母不是一件容易的事情，為什麼人們還是會選擇挑戰呢？一些父母接受了調查，研究人員問他們為什麼要生孩子，他們的答覆就列在下面。看看他們的回答，想想看，別人為什麼會選擇做父母？然後請記下你覺得當父母會碰到哪些有趣或困難的事情。如果你對養孩子這件事不了解，可以問問有經驗的爸爸媽媽們，請他們和你分享看法。請為各個分類想出至少四到五個可能的答案。

Parents' reasons for having children:

"I thought about the fun we would have together."

"I looked forwards to helping them grow into independent adults."

"Having children was a way of showing my love for my partner."

 完成句子。

Write your ideas about parenthood on the lines provided.

Enjoyable aspects of being a parent:

_____

_____

_____

_____

Difficult aspects of being a parent:

_____

_____

_____

_____

提示與解析

要記得，你日常生活中也有可能討論到這個話題，所以可以多練習說說你的想法，才能和別人在對話中分享意見，光會寫不會說是不夠的！舉例來說，如果你想講講你覺得當父母最困難或最有趣之處，你可以說：

One enjoyable aspect of being a parent is seeing my son / daughter grow up. Another enjoyable aspect is joining in his / her games. One difficult aspect of being a parent is trying to do everything properly. Another difficult aspect is always having to think about his / her needs.

因為你現在講的是個人意見，你也可以用這樣的句型來說：

In my opinion, one enjoyable aspect...
As far as I'm concerned, one difficult aspect...
If you ask me, another difficult aspect...

你覺得你會更容易想到育兒的有趣之處還是困難之處呢？

練習發表意見。

拒當英文句點王，換你練習開口說說看！

寫下自己的意見後，試著講出來，讓英語口語更流利！

Part 3——
社交英語無師自通，
道地的「照顧寶寶的事宜」該怎麼說？

十年英語不白學，
「照顧寶寶遇到的問題」就這麼說

接下來，請聆聽一位母親與一位育兒專家的對話。在這段對話中，你會聽到育兒專家莫琳（Maureen）問了那位母親許多問題。仔細聽聽是哪些問題以及莫琳究竟給了哪些意見。回答以下問題。

🔊 聽音檔並回答問題。　◀ *Track 012*

❶ The questions which the expert asks are ＿＿＿＿＿＿.

　　a. medical　　　　　　　b. technical

　　c. psychological　　　　d. general and practical

❷ Maureen gives only one piece of advice. What is it?

＿＿＿＿＿＿＿＿＿＿＿＿＿＿＿＿＿＿＿＿＿＿＿＿＿＿＿＿

提示與解析

雖然莫琳是心理學專家，但她並沒有問琳賽（Linsey）任何醫學的（medical）、專業的（technical）或心理的（psychological）問題。 她問的問題都很概括、很實際（如：寶寶幾歲、琳賽有哪些最大的煩惱），所以，第❶題的答案是最後一項。而她給了一個建議："...you really must get used to letting other people take some responsibility for her now and again". （你真的該習慣讓其他人偶爾幫你照顧寶寶。）

聽音檔並回答以下問題。 ◀ *Track 012*

① Notice that Maureen says「Many other young mothers would agree with you". She makes two other similar statements, which serve the same purpose. Listen carefully and complete the utterances below, writing down the exact words that Maureen says.

a. Yes, lots of women (9 words) _____

_____.

b. Yes, that's a (2 words) _____ at first.

② What is Maureen's purpose in making the remarks above? (Circle the best suggestion.)

a. To give advice.

b. To make Linsey feel better.

c. To tell Linsey what she should do.

e. To collect information for research purposes.

③ How can we summarise the expert's attitude? (Circle the best suggestion.)

a. The expert is being critical.

b. The expert is being reassuring.

c. The expert is being insistent.

d. The expert is being dismissive.

提示與解析

① a. feel like you after they have their first child
   b. natural reaction
② b
③ b (She's being reassuring. She wants to persuade Linsey that her reactions are normal.)

十年英語不白學，「描述寶寶」就這麼說

　　在兩人的對話中，談論到許多關於寶寶的資訊。再聽一遍音檔，記下對話中描述了寶寶的哪些事情。在沒有提到的項目旁打叉，提到的項目旁打勾，並把其中提到的資訊寫在旁邊。

🔊 完成表格。 🔈 *Track 012*

Aspects	√／✕	Specific information
birthplace		
age		
sex (M／F)		
name		
health		
height／length		
weight		
behaviour		

從對話中,我們無法得知寶寶的出生地(birthplace)、健康狀況(health)、身高 / 身長或體重(height / length or weight)。我們倒是可以聽出寶寶的年紀(almost 6 months)、名字(Clare)、表現(does not sleep very well)。至於寶寶的性別,兩人雖沒直接說出,但莫琳問了琳賽,"She's your first baby, isn't she?" 琳賽也說 "It isn't that I don't love her.",從代名詞 "she" 與 "her" 便可以看出寶寶的性別了。

順帶一提,英文中我們常會說寶寶的「身長」(length)而不說「身高」(height),因為寶寶嬰兒時期還站不起來,所以我們會說他 / 她有多「長」。

十年英語不白學,
「想表達情緒時」就這麼說

　　對話中的媽媽琳賽對於當媽這件事有很多的疑惑,對話中也有很多地方表達了這樣的意思。以下的句子是從對話中擷取的,但其中省略了表達琳賽情緒的部分。仔細聽音檔,將句子補充完整。

🔊 聽音檔,完成句子。　◀ *Track 012*

❶ I always thought I'd be quite a good parent but... I feel _____ _____.

❷ These six months have been _____ _____ _____ _____ of my life, and the most _____.

❸ Mainly just that I'm _____ _____ all the time.

❹ During the day, I _____ _____ _____ _____.

⑤ By the time I've taken care of all Clare's needs, there's _____ _____ _____ _____ _____ _____.

⑥ The house is _____ _____ and I always feel _____ _____.

⑦ My friend agreed to babysit—but, each time, I spent the whole evening _____ about whether Clare was OK!

⑧ I could do with her help and _____ now.

提示與解析

❶ very confused

❷ the longest six months; difficult

❸ so tired

❹ never have any energy

❺ no time left for anything else

❻ a mess; so disorganised

❼ worrying

❽ support

十年英語不白學，「提供建議」就這麼說

琳賽覺得自己是個不合格的母親，想要盡快解決問題。然而對話中，專家只給了她一個意見（前面的練習中可以看出這點）。那你呢？願不願意給琳賽一點意見？針對以下提到的問題，請從各選項中選擇適當的建議方式，或自己想一些其他的建議。請使用 "should + 原形動詞" 的句型。

 選擇或提供建議。

1 Linsey feels tired and disorganised all the time because of the baby care.
- She should insist that her husband should share the responsibility.
- She should hire a long-term babysitter to help her.
- She should ask her mother-in-law to help her with baby care.

2 She is going to send Clare to a childminder in three months.
- She should wait till the bay is older.
- She should spend as much time as possible with her child in the early stages so that they can bond.
- She should choose the childminder very carefully.

3 Linsey is going back to work soon.
- She shouldn't go back to work until her baby is two years old.
Your suggestion?

4 When Clare cries, Linsey always feeds her.
- She should try to find out the reason for crying.
- She should leave the baby to cry.
Your suggestion?

❺ Linsey keeps worrying about the baby if she and her husband go out in the evenings and leave the baby with friends.
  • She shouldn't worry so much.
  • She should trust other people.
Your suggestion?

❻ She's thinking of asking her mother to help with baby care but her mother lives up in Scotland, far away from her home.
  • Her mother should come to live together with them.
  • She and her baby should move to her mother's.
Your suggestion?

❼ She's beginning to think one child is enough. She doubts her love for the baby.
  • She should talk with experienced mothers and exchange ideas about this.
Your suggestion?

❽ Linsey is going to do a full-time job soon.
  • She should find a part-time job instead.
Your suggestion?

提示與解析

無論選哪個建議,只要能夠合理解釋,都是沒有問題的。你自己提出的建議也一樣,請注意使用正確的句型。

Part 4——
社交英語無師自通，
道地的「日常生活問題」該怎麼說？

在日常生活中，如果你遇到一些問題，例如小孩不喜歡上學、或面臨離婚困擾等，你該怎麼辦呢？你可能會和親朋好友聊一聊。但是你也可以到圖書館、書店或網路上找一本能幫你解決問題的書，現在這方面的書或文章有很多。

為什麼有些人寧可用讀書的方法，找到解決問題的方式，也不找人聊聊呢？想想看，你一定知道答案的。

以下的 Text 3 中包含八本書的簡介，這些書中提供的是解決親子關係、老年照護、各種歧視等問題的方法或建議。仔細閱讀描述，選擇最適合各篇文章的標題，要特別注意文章中的關鍵字（key words）。把你所選的標題寫在各段簡介上面的空白處。第一題已經為你做好了！

Titles

Helping Your Child to Live with Your Divorce

A Practical Guide to Choosing Child Care

Moving House: Helping Your Child Enjoy the Experience

Friends and Enemies: Childhood Relationships

A Practical Guide to Caring for the Elderly

Children Under Stress

An Equal Future: Anti-sexist Practice in the Early Years

A Practical Guide to Managing Stress

為各段描述選擇最合適的標題。

Text 3A

Friends and Enemies: Childhood Relationships

This book deals with general difficulties that arise in children's relationships with one another. The major issue explored is bullying. It is of major importance to both bullies and, especially, their victims, that everyone involved understands why it happens and how best to deal with it. Anyone who knows a child who suffers from being afraid of his / her friends or classmates will benefit from reading this helpful publication.

Text 3B

_____

Stress affects most people at some stage of their lives. This book helps you recognise early warning signals and analyse the problems that can cause stress both at home and at work. It suggests numerous ways of tackling the problems and reducing the burden on yourself.

Text 3C

_____

This book helps working parents face the issue of arranging satisfactory care for their young children. It clearly presents the options that are available and gives guidance to parents who are in need of securing financial assistance for the care of their children. Useful telephone numbers of agencies and support groups are included.

Text 3D

The various types of stress suffered by children are often very difficult to deal with. Children who live with disabled parents or siblings, who experience the death of a close relative or who witness the breakdown of their parents' relationship need help and understanding. This book offers practical advice on how best to offer support.

Text 3E

If you feel you have suffered from male / female inequalities and hope to ensure that your child escapes similar problems, this book is for you. It explores ways of extending opportunities for boys and girls in the early years and offers valuable advice on how to foster gender equality. It lays stress on the fact that anti-sexist practice early in a child's life will greatly enhance his / her chances of becoming a well-balanced adult.

Text 3F

Parents who are undergoing the stresses of divorce and separation are frequently so involved in their own problems that it is easy to overlook the consequent suffering of their children. This book offers a range of suggestions which will help you to work out the best strategies for protecting your child from unnecessary worries. It gives advice on helping with offspring of all ages—from very young babies to young adults.

Text 3G

This slim volume offers practical guidance on helping your child to cope with the problems associated with moving to a new place and changing school. Moving can be an upsetting experience for children. This booklet offers suggestions on minimising the sense of loss they feel when they say goodbye to familiar people and places, and gives advice on how to make the process of readjustment exciting rather than worrying.

Text 3H

This booklet is a valuable source of information about all aspects of caring for elderly relatives. It lists useful telephone numbers of government facilities and assistance, nursing services, support groups and so on. It presents helpful hints on making your home safer and more convenient for people with limited mobility and, perhaps most importantly, recommends strategies that will help you, the carer, cope with day-to-day stress levels.

提示與解析

Text 3B: A Practical Guide to Managing Stress
Text 3C: A Practical Guide to Choosing Child Care
Text 3D: Children Under Stress
Text 3E: An Equal Future: Anti-sexist Practice in the Early Years
Text 3F: Helping Your Child to Live with Your Divorce
Text 3G: Moving House: Helping Your Child Enjoy the Experience
Text 3H: A Practical Guide to Caring for the Elderly

你是如何選出適當的標題的呢？一定是在各段文章中抓到了一些關鍵字。請將幫助你選出正確標題的「關鍵字」寫在下列表格中。

寫出關鍵字或片語。

Texts	Key words / phrases
3A	*children's relationships, bullying*
3B	
3C	
3D	
3E	
3F	
3G	
3H	

提示與解析

- Text 3A 講的是孩子們在處理同伴關係時容易遇到的困難。關鍵字有：children's relationships, bullying等。
- Texts 3B、3D 和3F都和壓力有關，但討論的是不同種類的壓力。Text 3B討論的是大部分的人（尤其是成人）在一般日常生活中可能會遇到的壓力，並提出了解決的方法。關鍵字有：stress, tackle the problems, reduce the burden等。Text 3D則是討論孩子們遇到的壓力，並提供方法，幫助壓力大

Unit 1 Unit 2 Unit 3 Unit 4 人生百態 People

的孩子。關鍵字有：stress suffered by children, practical advice等。而 Text 3F，則是幫助孩子應對父母離婚、分居的壓力。關鍵字有：suffering of their children, protecting your child from unnecessary worries等。

- Text 3C 討論的則是各種不同的育兒方式。關鍵字有：satisfactory care for young children, options, care of their children等。
- Text 3E 說的是男女平等。關鍵字有：male / female inequalities, foster gender equality等。
- Text 3G 討論的是搬家可能會給孩子帶來的影響。關鍵字有：move, change, readjustment等。
- Text 3H 則討論照顧老年家屬或親人的各個方面。關鍵字有：care for elderly relatives, carer等。

十年英語不白學，「描述日常生活中遇到的問題」就這麼說

任何人在日常生活中都可能遇到問題。接下來，你會看到一些需要你幫助的人的狀況，從前面的書單中，推薦給他們適合的書。把適合的書籍的標題填在相應的表格中。

為需要幫助的人推薦書籍。

People with problems	Book recommended
Situation 1. Jessy has always felt she has been at a disadvantage because she is female and has lacked confidence as a result. She wants to make sure her children learn good strategies while they are still young.	

Situation 2. Allen is a boy of 11 years old. He is shy and unsociable. He is often beaten up by his classmates and gets into trouble at school. His parents are very worried about him.	
Situation 3. Davies, five, is a little "walking disaster". When he was four, he chopped the end of his finger off with a penknife and had to have it sewn back on. Last month, doctors had to stitch his head after he plunged headlong into a pool. His parents are worried about what will happen when his mother goes back to work and he has to be looked after by a childminder.	
Situation 4. The relationship between James and Lisa is getting worse. They seem to quarrel all the time. Their only daughter feels insecure at home and can't concentrate on her studies at school. As a result, she often plays in the park instead of going to school and has started to steal things from shops.	

提示與解析

Situation 1: An Equal Future: Anti-sexist Practice in the Early Years
Situation 3: A Practical Guide to Choosing Child Care

Situation 2: Friends and Enemies: Childhood Relationships
Situation 4: Helping Your Child to Live with Your Divorce

十年英語不白學，「簡單介紹書籍」就這麼說

　　在書籍的簡介中，常會看到一些實用的動詞或動詞片語。比如說：deal(s) with, present(s), list(s), recommend(s), explore(s), suggest(s), offer(s) / give(s) / provide(s) advice (or suggestions)等。請你利用在238頁到241頁中為每本書選擇的標題以及每本書的概略內容，簡單地為這些書寫個簡介。前四本只要完成以下句子就好，後面四本則請你自己寫出完整的句子。第一題已經為你做好了！

請為第一個練習中的每本書寫簡介。

3A: This book deals with *childhood relationships*. (a general topic)

It explores *the major issue of bullying*.

3B: This book deals with _____. (a general topic)

It offers advice on how to _____

3C: This book deals with _____. (a general topic)

It presents _____ and gives advice on _____.

3D: This book deals with _____. (a general topic)

It provides advice on how best to _____.

請為剩下的四本書寫下簡單的描述。

3E: _____

_____

3F: _____

_____

3G: _____

_____

3H: _____

_____

提示與解析

3B：This book deals with the ways of managing stress. It offers advice on how to tackle the problem and reduce the burden on yourself.

3C：This book deals with the care of young children. It presents options and gives advice on arranging satisfactory care for children.

3D：This book deals with children under stress. It provides advice on how best to offer support.

至於剩餘四本書的內容簡介，沒有標準答案，以下只是參考解答，你的答案不一定要和參考答案一模一樣，但一定要涵蓋到每本書的內容重點。

3E: This book deals with equality (and inequality). It offers valuable advice on how to foster gender equality early in a child's life.

3F: This book deals with helping children (or offspring) cope with their parents' divorce. It suggests a range of strategies for protecting children from unnecessary worries.

3G: This book deals with problems associated with moving house and changing school. It offers suggestions on minimising the sense of loss children feel when they leave a familiar place.

3H: This book deals with caring for the elderly. It recommends strategies that will help you, the carer, cope with stress.

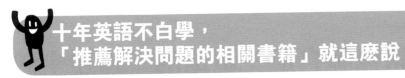

十年英語不白學，「推薦解決問題的相關書籍」就這麽說

再看一遍第一個練習中每本書籍的簡介，相信你會看到以下這些說法：

offer / give advice on
lay stress on
presents hints on
offer suggestions on

你有沒有發現這些說法都用了介系詞 "on" 呢？

This book offers practical advice on *how best to offer support*.
It lays stress on *the fact that anti-sexist practice*...
It presents helpful hints on *making your home*...
This booklet offers suggestions on *minimising the sense of loss*...

介系詞（preposition）後面一般要接名詞或名詞片語。這裡介系詞on後面出現了三種形式：

+ *the verb-ing*...
+ *how to*...
+ *noun*...

練習使用這樣的句型說說看。回頭看看第三個練習中的不同人面對的不同問題。想像一下，如果這些角色跑來跟你抱怨了他們面對的問題，而你要推薦一本書給他們，你會怎麽說？請使用上面講到的句型，完成下面的句子。

"You could read _____. It might help. It deals with _____. It offers advice on _____."

拒當英文句點王，換你練習開口說說看！

練習說說看。

Part 5──
社交英語無師自通，道地的「描述生活中的各種角色」該怎麼說？

十年英語不白學，
「描述各種角色」就這麼說

大家在生活中都得扮演某些角色，有些人甚至一人分飾多角。以下的 Text 4 描述的就是一個女性的各種角色。Text 4 其實是一封信，是寫給*Family World*《家庭世界》雜誌的，而這封信就刊登在雜誌的 "Your Views"（也就是讀者來信專欄）。快速閱讀一遍，大概了解一下寫信者的狀況。

快速閱讀文章，完成表格。

The writer's general situation
1. Marital status:
2. Number of children:
3. Present occupation:
4. Her problem / frustration:

Text 4

1. I wonder if any other readers who do not have a job feel as frustrated as I do by many people's responses. I am repeatedly asked "Why aren't you working?" and I feel this question is a criticism. People seem to be suggesting that I am lazy and useless, wasting my life "doing nothing". Is it so wrong to want to stay at home and take care of my home and family? I enjoy it and would like to remind all those women (and men!) who are critical of people like me that it is possible to stay at home and feel valued and fulfilled. My husband and two children really appreciate me, and the atmosphere in our house is happy and positive.

2. Luckily, my husband earns enough money to support us all but I believe that, in many ways, I save money by staying at home. If I had a job, I would need help with the children, the home and the garden. I would need to have a freezer to store food, have a food processor and a microwave cooker to save time. I would have to buy expensive convenience foods because I wouldn't have time to cook properly. I would have to pay babysitters and childminders, music teachers, hairdressers, gardeners, odd-job men and many others. And, the truth is, I do not want to pay other people to work for my family! I love being with them in all sorts of different situations.

3. My days are as busy and satisfying as those of most people who have jobs outside the home. As well as doing the usual cooking and cleaning, I make healthy and economical soups, jam, biscuits and cakes. I help my children with their homework and organise exciting games for them and their friends. I do all the household decorating and repairs. I make clothes for the whole family. And, what is more important, I have time to really talk to my husband and children.

4. Staying at home all day is not boring. I plan my time carefully so that I can attend courses at the local college and take part in local politics and charity work.

5. I would advise any parent who can afford it to stay at home. It is economically and psychologically wise to do so—if that's what you want. Perhaps some of my main critics are people who don't enjoy working at home for the family. I do not criticise people who choose to work. I just wish they would allow me to do as I choose. I am proud to be a housewife.

(Mary Jay, Birmingham)

從文中得知，這位女士已經結婚了，有兩個孩子。她是個家庭主婦，並沒有在外面賺錢，因此就有許多人認為她「沒有工作」。每次被人家問「你為什麼不工作？」她就很不開心，因為她覺得別人好像認為她懶惰又沒用。

答案：

1. married 2. two children 3. housewife
4. She was repeated asked by people why she wasn't working and people may suggest that she was lazy and useless.

一般而言，大部分的段落都會有關鍵句（或句子的一部分），可以涵蓋整個段落的內容。這樣的關鍵句就叫做 "topic sentence"，通常會是段落的第一句或最後一句。但也有時候，不會有真正的「關鍵句」，而只是在段落中有稍微「提示」一下整段內容的句子。

你覺得以下列出的句子是不是第2、3、4段的關鍵句呢？如果不是，請在文章中畫出你覺得是關鍵句的句子。

Para. 2 My husband earns enough money to support the whole family.

Para. 3 My days are as busy and satisfying as those of most people who have jobs outside the home.

Para. 4 Staying at home all day is not boring.

提示與解析

第3、4段的開頭句，確實就是整段的關鍵句。然而，第2段的開頭句並非關鍵句。仔細看第2段，大部分的內容都在講寫信人如何省錢，而不是講她老公怎麼賺錢。因此，正確的關鍵句應該是：I save money by staying at home.

十年英語不白學，「各種角色」就這麼說

在 Text 4 中，我們提到許多人認為寫信的這個女子是「沒有工作的」。你覺得呢？其實，她在家裡也是在工作，而且還省錢。在家裡，她扮演了許多角色是和「上班」無關的。我已經為你寫下第一個角色了。你知道她扮演的其他角色嗎？

將寫信者扮演的各種角色寫在下面。

a childminder / babysitter, _____

_____

_____

_____

_____

提示與解析

全文直接或間接地提到以下這些角色：a childminder / babysitter（保姆），a gardener（園丁），a cook（廚師），a music teacher / a teacher（音樂老師或老師），a hairdresser（理髮師），an odd-job man（打零工者，尤指在房子或花園裡工作者），a cleaner（清潔人員），a sports / games organiser（運動與遊戲規劃人員），a decorator（裝潢人員），a repairman（修理人員），a dressmaker / tailor（裁縫），a student（學生），a charity worker（慈善工作者）。

我們可以想像，這位媽媽應該還可能會扮演很多其他的角色，像是孩子生病的時候，她就要當 "doctor / nurse"（醫生或護士），而如果她想讓孩子開心，也可能扮演 "actress"（演員）或 "clown"（小丑）。

　　想想看，你在生活中扮演了哪些角色呢？想到我們每天都用到這麼多不同的「技能」，很為自己感到自豪吧。

　　你注意到 "odd-job man" 和 "repairman" 這兩個角色了嗎？雖然這位媽媽是女性，但我們不需要說 "odd-job woman" 或 "repairwoman"。有些人覺得全都說 "man" 對女性不公平，所以也可以說 "odd-job person" 或 "repair person"。

十年英語不白學，
「不用外出工作的好處和壞處」就這麼說

　　以下列出了不外出工作的好處與壞處。請從中選出所有的好處（advantages），在旁邊寫 "A"。再選出所有的壞處（disadvantages），在旁邊寫下 "D"。

判斷以下句子是不外出工作的好處還是壞處，並分別標出來。

❶ If a parent is a full-time househusband / housewife, he / she can save money.

❷ If a parent does not have to go out to work, he / she can also feel satisfied and fulfilled.

❸ If a parent does not have a job, he / she can feel isolated from other people.

❹ If a parent only works at home, he / she can become too concerned about domestic details.

❺ If a parent doesn't have a job, he / she can spend more time with his / her children.

⑥ If a parent does not earn his / her own salaries, he / she will have to be financially dependent on his / her partner.

⑦ If a parent doesn't have a paid job, he / she can create a happy atmosphere for the family.

⑧ If a parent is at home all day, he / she can have lots of energy for his / her family.

⑨ If a parent doesn't go out to work, he / she can spend time preparing healthy food for the family.

⑩ If a parent stays at home all day, he / she will become lazy and boring.

提示與解析

Advantages：①, ②, ⑤, ⑦, ⑧, ⑨
Disadvantages: ③, ④, ⑥, ⑩

十年英語不白學，
「表達自己的看法」就這麼說

你對於家庭主婦和家庭主夫有什麼看法呢？你覺得父母應該辭職在家照顧年幼兒童嗎？看看上一個練習中的說法，你覺得哪些才是你的看法呢？請注意句型：

If + Present Simple, Future Simple
                OR
If + Present Simple, can + 原形動詞

一旦你確定了上一個練習中哪些句子可以代表你的想法，請用同樣的句型寫下三個句子，以表達你對此話題的其他看法。你可以說優點也可以說缺點。

寫下三個句子，表達你的看法。

❶ _____

_____

_____

❷ _____

_____

_____

❸ _____

_____

_____

提示與解析

這個練習沒有標準答案，不過建議你練習大聲把自己寫下的句子說出來，和別人討論到這個話題時也可以拿出來分享。

Part 6——
社交英語無師自通，
道地的「不同的態度」該怎麼說？

十年英語不白學，
「判斷別人的態度」就這麼說

　　你會發現，我們之前的練習中辨別在家裡照顧孩子的好處和壞處時，用的是 "parent" 這個詞，而不是 "mother"。為什麼呢？因為雖然過去大家總認為在家裡照顧孩子、做家務的應該是媽媽，但現在我們明白，爸爸一樣也可以待在家裡照顧孩子，不一定非得由媽媽來做。因此，隨著社會的發展，大家要注意避開各種帶有性別歧視的字詞了。

　　接下來，請聽音檔，聽一聽一位英國女性談她的想法。聽第一遍時，先試著判斷她大概的態度。以下提供一些可能的形容詞，請從中選出最符合她態度的單字。如果你對某些字不太熟悉，可以先查一下字典。

🔊 聽音檔，選出符合說話者態度的形容詞。　🔊 *Track 013*

egalitarian	*traditional*	*unusual*
typical	*modern*	*unrealistic*

提示與解析

這位女士肯定不是一個 "traditional"（傳統的）的人吧！大部分的人都會覺得她的看法很現代，那她的態度屬於 "unusual"（少見的）還是 "typical"（典型的）呢？在一些比較傳統的地方，肯定會覺得她的想法比較少見，但在日漸現代化的社會中，許多人也都開始接受這樣的看法了。這裡沒有正確答案，只要你能夠合理解釋你的看法即可。不過，我們可以確定，說話者的看法是屬於 "egalitarian"（平等主義的）的。

十年英語不白學，「表達支持和反對的態度」就這麼說

再聽一遍音檔，判斷以下的句子是否符合說話者的看法。在符合的句子前面打勾。要特別注意，以下列出的句子都在音檔中出現過，你必須根據上下文判斷說話者在講出這些句子時，是持支持態度還是反對態度。

🔊 聽音檔，選擇代表說話者看法的句子。 ◀ Track 013

❶ Some roles are more suitable for males than females.

❷ Men and women are equally capable of learning all skills.

❸ Parents should share household tasks.

❹ The division of labour should depend on individual circumstances.

❺ We can learn most things if we try.

❻ Women should take care of most of the practical aspects of childcare.

❼ They (women) are more gentle, more patient and more skilled.

❽ Men are physically stronger than women.

❾ Men are better at doing certain types of physical work.

❿ Cleaning, washing and ironing are "women's work".

⓫ There's no such thing as "women's work".

⓬ A man shouldn't do the ironing.

符合說話者想法：**2** , **3** , **4** , **5** , **8** , **9** , **11**
不符合說話者想法：**1** , **6** , **7** , **10** , **12**

十年英語不白學，「表達意見」就這麼說

在上面的練習中，說話者在說出這些句子前，用了怎樣的句型呢？舉例來說，說話者一開始說 "men and women are equal"（男女平等）時，前面還加上了 "It is my firm belief that..."（我堅信……）。

🔊 聽音檔，寫下上面練習中說話者表達意見時用到的句型。

◀ *Track 013*

❶ I cannot accept that...
❷ As far as I'm concerned...
❸ In my view,...
❹ I think...
❺ It seems to me that...
❻ It's unwise to suggest that...
❼ I acknowledge that...
❽ I don't deny...
❾ I reject the suggestion that...
❿ I strongly believe that...
⓫ If you ask me...

你會發現，以上列出的句型，有些代表同意，有些則代表反對。舉例來說，"I cannot accept that..." 通常是用來表示「這個看法很多人都接受，但我不接受」的態度。而 "I reject the suggestion that..." 表達了同樣激烈的反對之意。

練習利用上面的句型，說說自己的看法。想像一下，如果你正在和這位說話者聊天，你會對她說什麼？你會反對她的看法嗎？練習說說看，也可以找朋友一起討論。討論完後，把自己的看法寫在下方。

寫下表達你個人看法的句子。

Part 7——
社交英語無師自通，道地的「描述問題和提供解決辦法」該怎麼說？

**十年英語不白學，
「描述問題和提供解決辦法」就這麼說**

　　以下的 Text 5 擷取自一本雜誌的「建議」小專欄。這是什麼樣的專欄呢？這種專欄在雜誌上常見到，讀者可以將自己的煩惱寫信投稿，由心理、醫學、育兒等各界專家或人生經驗豐富者為他們解惑。通常這種專欄占據版面不大，或許只有一頁，所以英文稱為 "Problem Page"。我們接下來要看到的 Text 5 就是來自 "Dear Lucy" 專欄。負責這個專欄的人叫露西（Lucy），因此讀者寫信給她求助時，就會以 "Dear Lucy..." 當開頭。聽起來很親切吧！正是因為這樣，讀者才會更願意與她分享他們的私人問題。

　　一般而言，在這些讀者的來信之後就會直接放上露西的回覆，但在這裡我們稍微改變一下做法，先將五封讀者來信放在一起（Text 5），之後的 Text 6 才列出露西的回答。請快速閱讀 Text 5 與 Text 6，將來信與回信配成對。請注意，其中有一封信並沒有收到回覆。在以下的方框中填入正確的字母，請在沒有回覆的那封信旁打叉。

 請將來信與回信搭配起來。

Letter	**Reply**
Mother-in-law drives me mad:	
Father fears:	
Bullying son:	
Nosy neighbour:	
Daughter worry:	

Text 5

Dear Lucy...
Your problems answered by
Dr. Lucy Fable

1. MOTHER-IN-LAW DRIVES ME MAD!

I've been happily married for nine years and have two lovely children. My problem is my mother-in-law. She's so critical of everything I do: the way I take care of the children, the things I buy and the food I cook. My husband is a quiet, easy-going guy and he's always telling me that I should just ignore her unkind remarks. I've been trying to do that ever since I met her but I now feel I'm going to explode one day. We're very close family and I don't want to cause a family row but she makes me feel so angry and humiliated. What can I do?

2. FATHER FEARS

My mum died ten years ago and we invited my dad to come and live with us. He refused because we live in another town and he couldn't face leaving his old friends and so on. He managed very well alone until recently. I visit him at least every two weeks and I've started to notice that he's getting quite forgetful, often leaving the gas on, burning pans and so on. I'm worried about him and phone him several times each day to check that he's all right. I'm afraid he's no longer fit to take care of himself. What shall I do?

3. BULLYING SON

I've been told by a friend that my teenage son has been bullying younger children at school. He seems such a quiet boy but has never had many close friends. I find it hard to believe he would behave like this but I'm sure my friend is telling the truth. How should I deal with the problem?

4. NOSY NEIGHBOUR

My neighbour is a middle-aged widow who lives alone. She spends hours in our house every day and frequently interferes in how we take care of the children. She's always giving them sweets and ice cream and, when we scold them, she tells them we're only joking. It's driving my husband and me crazy. How can I tell her she visits too often?

5. DAUGHTER WORRY

My 24-year-old daughter has always been shy and boys were rarely interested in her. Ten months ago she started going out with a man who is just the opposite of her: loud, big-headed and very bad with money. At first I thought he would be good for her confidence and I felt sure she would quickly tire of him. Now she has informed me that they are planning to get married. I'm so upset because I am sure she is making a big mistake and I know he'll make a dreadful husband. My daughter just won't listen to me. How can I make her see sense? What can I do to stop her?

Text 6

6A.

This is a classic situation in which your kindness has brought you problems! If I were you, I would tackle one issue at a time. You must start by being firm. Instead of allowing her to drop in any time, you should fix times when it's convenient. Then, a while later, tell her she should not give the children sweets more than once a week. Next, try to explain that she must not interfere when you scold them. She should slowly take the hint. If she doesn't, simply repeat the message!

6B.

Your problem is a common one but that fact doesn't make it any easier to tackle. If you don't do something soon, I'm afraid you will explode! So, it's important to deal with the problem. You should start by believing that you have the right to hold your own opinions and that you are a good wife and mother. Then, the main thing is to remain calm. When she is critical, look her in the eye and point out that you have different ways of doing things and remind her that her son and grandchildren are well and happy (so you must be doing some things right!). Whatever you do, don't get angry because you are likely to regret it if you do. It sounds hard but it will get easier as soon as you start to do something other than silently seething.

6C.

Many mothers feel unhappy about the partners their children choose. You cannot stop your daughter's marriage! Your fears about her boyfriend may be correct but you should remember that your daughter is no longer a child. Her opinions count too. She may enjoy the balance that her boyfriend provides and feel that his loudness makes up for her shyness. If I were you, I would try to talk sensibly with her and find out whether she really loves him. You could ask her how she imagines she will deal with the fact that he's not too good with money and so on. Listen to her carefully. She probably understands the problems better than you do. She's old enough to make up her own mind, so don't risk losing her trust by being critical of her future partner.

6D.

So many people experience your problem when they live miles away from their old parents. If I were you, I'd repeat the suggestion that your father should move in with you. He may have changed his mind without even realising it himself! If he's still determined not to move to an unfamiliar town, you should start looking at the nursing homes that are available in his area. You could take your father to look at different homes so that he feels he's involved in the decision-making process. Talk to him about all the advantages of such places (the company, the convenience, the comfort, etc.) and convince him that you will still visit him as often as possible. The move will not be easy but putting it off may cause further problems. I'm sending you our "Caring for the Elderly" leaflet.

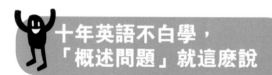

十年英語不白學，「概述問題」就這麼說

每封信的標題都簡略地說明了每個寫信者遇到的難題。仔細看看每封信，找出能夠概括整個問題的句子。

 寫下能夠概括整個問題的句子。

❶ _____

❷ _____

❸ _____

❹ _____

❺ _____

④ She spends hours in our house every day and frequently interferes in how we take care of the children.

⑤ I'm sure she's making a big mistake and I know he'll make a dreadful husband.

 十年英語不白學，
「使用祈使句提供解決辦法」就這麼說

這些寫信者都希望得到露西的建議。閱讀露西對前兩封信的回覆，仔細記下她提供的所有建議。請使用祈使句。

 寫下露西的建議。

❶ Mother-in-law drives me mad:

a. *Do something soon.*

b. *Deal with the problem.*

c. _____

d. _____

e. _____

f. _____

g. _____

h. _____

❷ Father fears:

a. *Repeat the suggestion that your father should move in with you.*

b. _____

c. _____

d. _____

e. _____

第一封信：

c. Start by believing that you have the right to hold your own opinions.

d. Remain calm.

e. Look her in the eye.

f. Point out that you have different ways of doing things.

g. Remind her that her son and grandchildren are well and happy.

h. Don't get angry.

第二封信：

b. Start looking at (the) nursing homes (that are available in his area).

c. Take your father to look at different homes.

d. Talk to him about all the advantages of such places.

e. Convince him that you will still visit him as often as possible.

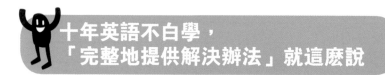

十年英語不白學，「完整地提供解決辦法」就這麼說

　　你應該發現了，光是用祈使句，可能很難涵蓋全部的建議。請看看下面列出的用來回覆第四、五封信的建議。這些建議出現在回信中的哪些地方呢？露西是怎麼說的？把她的建議完整地寫在下面。

 寫下露西回覆第四、五封信的完整建議。

Nosy neighbour:

ⓐ one issue at a time

_____

b be firm

_____

c times convenient

_____

d sweets not more than once a week

_____

e not interfere / scold

_____

f repeat message

_____

Daughter worry:

a daughter no longer a child

_____

b talk sensibly

_____

c deal with the fact of not too good with money

_____

d listen

_____

e risk losing her trust

_____

提示與解析

Nosy neighbour:
a If I were you, I would tackle one issue at a time.
b You must start by being firm.
c You should fix times when it's convenient.
d Tell her she should not give the children sweets more than once a week.

ⓔ Try to explain that she must not interfere when you scold them.

ⓕ If she doesn't (take the hint), repeat the message.

Daughter worry:

ⓐ You should remember that your daughter is no longer a child.

ⓑ If I were you, I would try to talk sensibly with her.

ⓒ You could ask her how she imagines she will deal with the fact that he's not too good with money.

ⓓ Listen to her carefully.

ⓔ Don't risk losing her trust by being critical of her future partner.

我們會發現，給人建議時，經常用到以下這些句型：

> Imperative form （祈使句）
>
> You must + 原形動詞
>
> You should + 原形動詞
>
> You could + 原形動詞
>
> If I were you, I would + 原形動詞

其中，祈使句（imperative form）當然是最直接的。這個句型可以讓露西的建議聽起來更清楚、更有力。

"must + 原形動詞" 也很有力，而 "should + 原形動詞" 語氣上則緩和一些。"could + 原形動詞" 以及 "If I were you..."（如果我是你的話……）的語氣更加親和，聽起來像是在給予建議而非命令。至於 "don't + 原形動詞"，聽起來則有點像是「警告」。

要記得，雜誌上的「建議」小專欄一般都很親切，並且令人信任、放心。雖然露西並不認識寫信的人，但她還是用一種很親密的態度來回信。

Part 8——
社交英語無師自通，
道地的「針對問題提供適合的解決辦法」該怎麼寫？

現在整個單元已經結束了！這個單元談論了很多問題，現在請再復習一遍整個單元，把你不懂的地方記下來，可以和同學、朋友互相討論。

學完這一單元，你就可以：

☐ 談論親子方面的話題。

☐ 看懂書籍大綱。

☐ 為書籍內容寫一個大綱。

☐ 推薦書籍。

☐ 描述角色。

☐ 表達態度與個人意見。

☐ 敘述優缺點。

☐ 描述問題。

☐ 提供建議。

第三封信目前並沒有收到回覆。你覺得露西會如何回覆這封信呢？再閱讀一遍這封信，想出四到五條可以給寫信者的建議，並寫一封「回信」。請使用前面介紹過的句型，用以下句子開頭：

"Your problem is quite a common one among parents of teenage children."

在作業本上寫一封回信。

使用以下標題：

Dealing with Your Bullying Son

第四單元總復習

**十年英語不白學，
「處理兩難的情況」就這麼說**

李晶正在和她的朋友瑪麗（Mary）談論一個困難的抉擇。

請聽她們的對話，在以下的表格中做筆記。 ◀ *Track 014*

Your Notes

Li Jing's promotion	
Her husband's situation	
Her company's reaction if she refuses	
Her daughter's situation	
Her parents-in-law's situation	
Why she wants the job	
Her final decision	
Her reasons	

| 271

Your Notes

Li Jing's promotion	Regional Director, based in Shenzhen
Her husband's situation	won't want to leave his job, also won't want to leave his parents and fail to carry out his duty to look after them
Her company's reaction if she refuses	will see it as lack of ambition, probably won't offer any promotion again
Her daughter's situation	four years old, needs looking after, would miss her grandparents if left
Her parents-in-law's situation	getting old, dependent on their son
Why she wants the job	previous Regional Director is not good, knows she could do the job better, fears another person getting it, also much more money
Her final decision	refuse the promotion
Her reasons	doesn't want to abandon her family, won't give up her family life for her job

 當你完成這個練習之後，試著用自己的觀點回答以下問題。

❶ Do you have any other advice you could give to Li Jing?

❷ What would you do in her situation?

❸ Do you think she made the right decision?

MP3音檔內容完整看

若是聽完音檔還是沒把握，建議可搭配本部份學習，不熟的語彙要查辭典並作筆記，方能加深英文記憶。

Maureen: How are you getting on?

Linsey: Well, not very well, I'm afraid. Motherhood is so different from how I imagined. I always thought I'd be quite a good parent but I feel... I don't know. I feel very confused.

Maureen: How old's your baby now?

Linsey: She's almost six months. These six months have been the longest six months of my life, and the most difficult.

Maureen: Yes! Many other young mothers would agree with you. It can be quite a shock... suddenly having another person to take care of. She's your first baby, isn't she?

Linsey: Yes, that's right. I used to think I'd like to have four or five children but I'm beginning to think one child is enough. It isn't that I don't love her. It's just, just...

Maureen: Yes, lots of women feel like you after they have their first child but they soon change their minds. The first few months are often the most difficult. You have to make so many adjustments to your life. What's your biggest worry?

Linsey: Mainly just that I am so tired all the time. Clare doesn't sleep very well so I have to get up lots of times during the night. Then, during the day, I never have any energy. By the time I've taken care of all Clare's needs, there's no time left for anything else. The house is a mess and I always feel so disorganised.

Maureen: I take it that you're still on maternity leave?

Linsey: Yes. I start work again in three months' time. Clare will go to a childminder. I really don't know how I'm going to manage to do a full-time job and be a good mother.

Maureen: I'm sure you'll manage perfectly. Does anyone help you with Clare at the moment?

Linsey: Umm... my husband tries to help when he can, but he works so hard that he's always very tired in the evenings when he gets home.

Maureen: So, you've been with Clare constantly since she was born?

Linsey: Almost, yes. Donald and I have tried to go out a couple of times. My friend agreed to babysit—but, each time, I spent the whole evening worrying about whether Clare was OK!

Maureen: Yes, that's a natural reaction at first, but you really must get used to letting other people take some responsibility for her now and again.

Linsey: I know, I know. That's what my mum keeps saying.

Maureen: Does your mum live near you?

Linsey: No, unfortunately. She lives up in Scotland at the moment. She spent three weeks with us after the birth and that was marvelous. I could do with her help and support now.

Maureen: I'm sure you could. It always helps to have a close family member around to help out. Do you have anyone like that near you?

Linsey: No relatives but I do have a couple of very good friends who try to help me. They each have two children so they're experienced mothers and can give me useful advice and listen to my problems.

 **Part 6: Track 013** （請配合255-257頁及音檔使用）

It is my firm belief that men and women are equal. I cannot accept that some roles are more suitable for males than for females. As far as I am concerned, men and women are equally capable of learning all skills. In my view, parents should share household tasks and childcare. I think the division of labour should depend on individual circumstances. It seems to me that we can learn most things if we try. It's unwise to suggest that women should take care of most of the practical aspects of childcare because they are more patient, more gentle and more skilled at it. Men can be just as skilled in these areas if they have practice! Of course, I acknowledge that men are often physically stronger than women and are therefore better at doing certain types of physical work. And I don't deny that one individual may be better at cooking, for example, than another. But I reject the suggestion that cleaning, washing and ironing are women's work. I strongly believe that we should question all types of sexual stereotyping. If you ask me, there's no such thing as "women's work". There's no reason at all why a man shouldn't do the ironing! My husband does all the ironing in our house—and I do all the electrical repairs!

A Personal Dilemma

Li Jing: Oh, Mary, I wonder if I could ask your advice about something.

Mary: Yes, of course. What is it?

Li Jing: Well, I have this dilemma, you see, that my company wants to promote me to Regional Director.

Mary: Oh, but that's great news! Congratulations!

Li Jing: Well, the problem is that it means moving to Shenzhen. That's where our regional headquarters are, so I'd have to work there.

Mary: Ah, and you're worried about your family.

Li Jing: Yes. You see, I know that my husband won't want to leave his job here. He tried a long time to get the job he really wants and he's very happy with this one. Then, there's my daughter. She's only four, so she really needs looking after.

Mary: Mm... I see your problem. Well, what would happen if you didn't take the job?

Li ling: Oh, I know my company. They would never offer me promotion again. In their view it would mean that I didn't have enough ambition. You know I suffered a lot under the previous Regional Director, and I'm now so glad that he's leaving. I know, if I were in the job I would do it much better than he did. But if someone else gets it, then I could go through all the same problems. I would really love to take it. Of course it would mean much more money too.

Mary: Is there any way you could take your daughter with you?

Li Jing: No, I wouldn't have time to look after her and she would get lonely without her grandparents. You see, my parents-in-law spend a lot of time with her, but they're getting old now and they won't be able to do too much in the future.

Mary: Are you sure your husband wouldn't want to move there with you?

Li Jing: Oh no. Apart from his work, he wouldn't like to leave his parents. He sees it as his duty to look after them. He goes to see them every day, does their shopping, takes them to the doctor when they need it. You see, they are really dependent on him.

Mary: Well, it looks like you have to make the decision between your job and your family—that's a hard one.

Li Jing: Oh, I know. In fact, I know what my decision has to be. I couldn't go off and abandon my daughter and my husband. My work is important to me, but not so much that I want to ruin my family life. I suppose I will just have to explain things to my boss and ask him to keep me in mind for anything that comes up locally.

Mary: Well, your company obviously thinks you're good enough for this job, so I don't think they will waste you. I'm sure they know how valuable you are to them. They'll probably offer you something else soon.

Li Jing: Well, we'll see. Anyway, thank you for letting me think aloud. I think I just needed to put my thoughts in order.

Mary: Oh, any time. I'm glad if I have been of some assistance.

NOTE

語研力 *E065*

引導式英語練習班：
聽說讀寫大量多元習題，打造英語力

勾勒回憶打底 → 激增擴展學習 → 定植永久記憶，學習省力也更有效率！

作　　者	顧曰國◎主編
顧　　問	曾文旭
出版總監	陳逸祺、耿文國
主　　編	陳蕙芳
執行編輯	翁芯俐
內文排版	李依靜
封面設計	李依靜
法律顧問	北辰著作權事務所

印　　製	世和印製企業有限公司
初　　版	2022 年 04 月

（本書改自《10年英語不白學，社交英語無師自通》）

出　　版	凱信企業集團 - 凱信企業管理顧問有限公司
電　　話	（02）2773-6566
傳　　真	（02）2778-1033
地　　址	106 台北市大安區忠孝東路四段 218 之 4 號 12 樓
信　　箱	kaihsinbooks@gmail.com

定　　價	新台幣 349 元 / 港幣 116 元
產品內容	1 書

總 經 銷	采舍國際有限公司
地　　址	235 新北市中和區中山路二段 366 巷 10 號 3 樓
電　　話	（02）8245-8786
傳　　真	（02）8245-8718

國家圖書館出版品預行編目資料

引導式英語練習班-聽說讀寫大量多元習題，打造
英語力／顧曰國著. – 初版. – 臺北市 : 凱信企業集
團凱信企業管理顧問有限公司, 2022.04
　面；　公分
ISBN 978-626-7097-13-7(平裝)

1.CST: 英語 2.CST: 會話

805.188　　　　　　　　　　111003843